The Overlords

St. Louis

By Robert Whitmore
Edited by Marie Joiner
Copyright 2024

Kenny McClelland walked out onto his balcony, overlooking the Chicago lakefront. He checked on the English Ivy, which grew along the top of the half-wall enclosing the space. The start of the ivy had been a gift from his father. He kept it trimmed meticulously to avoid letting it grow on the building itself.

A light wind came in off Lake Michigan. Kenny turned his gaze to the east, where the Sun had just broken the horizon. This was his favorite part of the morning. Steam rolled off his mug of tea. He took a sip without taking his eyes off the serene view.

He was looking forward to three or four days of rest after coming back from a culling trip to Duluth. Some of his peers enjoyed that part of the job, but Kenny viewed it as nothing more than maintaining his territory. Three thousand carefully selected humans had been brought to his plant near Lake Superior to be killed and processed. The resulting meat would then be shipped off to other territories as food for soldiers and commoners.

Sourcing meat from other territories was important for providing a variety of nutrients, so his deputies regularly ordered meat from other territories which would arrive at his ports in Chicago, Duluth, and Detroit on a weekly basis. His cargo trains would then carry the highly sought after sustenance to his own residents across the land that covered most of Michigan, Wisconsin, Minnesota, Missouri, Illinois, Iowa, and Indiana.

"Everything ok, sir?" asked Marie, Kenny's top aide. She stood in the doorway to the balcony wearing jeans, boots, and a solid black parka with a fur-lined hood pulled up over her head.

"Do you ever simply look down at the streets and watch them moving back and forth? They have their own tasks and such, but none of it matters."

"Sometimes," she said. "It does put more money in your pocket, though."

Kenny laughed and said, "As if I need more of that."

"True."

"To answer your question, I'm doing fine. There are any number of other things I'd rather spend my time on, but the Council insists on us personally overseeing the culls."

"I would be happy to do that for you," she said, showing the elongated canines in her upper row of teeth. Many people called them fangs, but that oversimplified their purpose and significance.

"I know you would. You might like it a bit too much," Kenny said, turning to look at her. The cold didn't bother him as much, so he wore only a blue button-down shirt with gray suit pants. His jacket and tie had been discarded on the ride home.

"Perhaps."

"You know I can feel you staring at my ears."

"Sorry, sir."

"What's with the 'sir' stuff, anyway? Something wrong?"

"All is well at last check."

He turned back to look at the lake and said, "You know these ears are sometimes a blessing and other times a curse. Sure, they let everyone know I'm genetically qualified to be an Overlord, but they also put a lot of attention on me."

"I wonder what it would be like sometimes. That's all."

"I'd say you are in the prime position," he said before taking a sip of his Vintage Narcissus tea. He had never taken a liking to coffee but had come across this tea on a visit to the Wuyi Mountains of China in the late 1700s. It was delicious tea. However, the fact it cost over three thousand dollars per pound made it taste better to him. "You don't have the pressure of being an Overlord and you aren't a Nomad, waiting for a chance to earn a territory of your own. Most of us never make it through the competitions."

"How long have you been an Overlord?"

"You've been with me for fifty years and that is the first time you've asked that," he said. "Most of my chief aides ask that within the first few years."

"I guess it never occurred to me to ask."

"Not a bad thing. Let's see," he said, taking another sip. "I've been in this role for close to seven hundred years. I was a Nomad for about a hundred before that. When this part of the world started growing and the Council started dividing up the continent, I earned my spot."

"Seven hundred years?"

"Yes. You do realize that we live longer than you, right?"

"I did know that, I guess. I haven't met many other Overlords though. Most of the ones I know are maybe three hundred years old. One grew up not too far from me."

"Carolina Garza?"

"That's her. She has a small territory in Southern California, Arizona, and Baja California."

"I've been there, but well before she was in charge. Neither of her parents were Overlords, right?"

"Nope, just commoners like me. Were your parents Overlords?"

"Oh, yes. Both of them. That added to my pressure to earn a territory. My dad has the British Isles, and my mother has most of Italy and Switzerland."

"They're still alive?"

Kenny snorted, shook his head, and took a long drink.

"They are very much alive and, if you ever meet them, don't comment on their age. Dad is about twelve hundred and my mom is close to two thousand."

"Whoa."

"How old do you think Queen Stephanie's council members are?"

"Never really thought about it."

"Let's just say the youngest is closing in on four thousand and Her Highness is rumored to be at least ten thousand years old. No one else has been around long enough to verify her age and no one would dare challenge her."

"I guess I have a lot to learn."

"Yes, but you've got time. Also, I'd be willing to bet the Overlords you know are older than you think."

"Maybe so," Marie said. "Can I make you another cup of tea... Kenny?"

"Please do. I'm going to go downstairs to check my email."

"I can put an app on your phone for that, if you want."

"No thanks. I don't need all that noise in my pocket."

"Very good, sir."

"Get out of here," he said and handed her his cup.

Marie spun and went to the kitchen. Kenny went down the spiral oak staircase that led to the lower floor, where he entertained guests and handled business. His art collection hung along both sides of the long hall at the center of that floor. He owned original Picasso, van Gogh, and O'Keefe works among many others.

At the base of the stairs, he paused to appreciate one of his Claude Monet paintings. His favorite was one of the famous water lily paintings because it had been a personal gift to him from the artist, who was a commoner.

Kenny turned left to go back under the staircase and into a narrow hallway that would lead past the second kitchen. Along the western end of the floor were his office and two meeting rooms. The whole complex was secured, but those rooms were only accessible by Kenny and Marie.

"All right," he said as he plopped down in his oversized leather desk chair. "What kind of stupid do I have waiting for me today?"

He gave his mouse two clicks to wake up the computer and then waited. That's when Brewster, his cat, emerged from his napping spot under an antique display cabinet filled with some of his favorite shoes.

Brewster weaved his way across the room with a serious look on his face. He was black with a white belly and a narrow white stripe up the middle of his face. Kenny was watching him when the email notification came up and he saw it was over a hundred. He sighed, thinking that he hadn't been gone that long.

"Looks like two new orders for Mitchell down in Louisiana. His team sure loves to eat, but that's good for me. I think I can pull together a delivery from western Missouri and Iowa without a problem. Shoot 'em right down the Mississippi."

"Knock, knock," Marie said in a sing-song voice, as she opened the door to the office. "I've got your tea."

"Come on in, but you don't have to knock or whatever you call that. I could hear you in the kitchen and walking down the hallway."

"Just being polite."

"Yes, I appreciate that, but it's unnecessary. Have a seat."

"What's bothering you?" she asked, and Brewster took up a spot on the floor halfway between them. He looked at her disapprovingly, but that's how he looked at everyone.

"Too many emails," he said. "I miss the old days. I had deputies in charge of the different parts of my territory. I would go around by train or coach and check on operations. It was easy and relaxing. Now, I have to carry a phone with me and stare at a computer for hours on end."

"The struggles of being you," Marie said.

"Your sarcasm is not wasted on me," he said, offering a slight smile. "You remind me a bit of my cousin, Melinda."

"Was she an Overlord?"

"Definitely not. A sort of an outcast in the family."

"Okay, well, thanks."

"She was pretty cool as far as I'm concerned. We had some good adventures."

"But she was nothing special?"

"On the contrary, she was very special. She just wasn't an Overlord. I'll tell you more sometime."

"That sounds good to me."

"Right now, I need to get back to these emails."

"I'll leave you to it," Marie said and turned toward the door. "Can I get you something to eat?"

"Not right now," Kenny said and scrolled through another half dozen emails. "Have you gotten a call from Paul?"

"Not since you left. Why?"

"I've received six emails from him."

"Want me to call him?"

"No. I'll do it," he said and took out his phone. "Could you get me some liver pâté?"

"That's so gross."

"With some Ritz crackers."

"Really?"

"Yes."

"What kind of liver?"

"Spanish would be nice. Portuguese is also good."

"I think we have Spanish," Marie said.

"Thank you," he said and tapped Paul's name on the phone. The phone rang once.

"Hey there, boss man! I was wondering when you would call."

"Did you try calling me?"

"Nope, but I sent a bunch of emails. I knew you were on a trip."

"And you know that I don't check my emails when I'm gone."

"Right! I forgot all about that."

Kenny sighed and said, "Is something wrong? I could've come straight to you in St. Louis, instead of stopping here."

"Wrong? Well, sort of," Paul said, clearing his throat. "We've got a group of people trying to organize some criminal activity. Wasn't sure how we should handle them."

"Come on, Paul. I should've left you out in the hills of southern Missouri. You know the key is determining if it's an actual threat to order. I have a lot of cities to maintain and that's why I have deputies."

"I'm trying! You know that."

"I think you are, yes. Just not sure it's enough for the role you're in."

"Let me explain, all right."

"Please do."

"So, this new group of guys is pretty organized. Haven't seen anything like it in a while. Probably back to the Capone days."

"And? Those guys were barely worth paying attention to."

"Sure, but these guys call themselves the Dracs."

"Cute."

"They are telling people they are vampires and that they're in charge. People know who we are from the stories and are letting these guys have more space to do their thing based on that. Not sure how far they'll push it."

"Okay, Paul. You did fine. I do wish you had called me instead of sending emails."

"Next time, I will."

"Let's hope it's a good long while before that," Kenny said and rocked back in his chair. He turned to look out across the city and thought about his options.

"Boss?"

"I'm here. Just thinking."

"Okay. I'm having a snack."

"Sounds about right," Kenny said. "I want you to find out whatever you can about these Dracs. Where is their headquarters? Who's in charge? How many people? All the basics. I'll be there as soon as I can."

"We can handle that," Paul said through a mouth full of food.

"Good," Kenny said and hung up.

Marie had come back in for the last part of that conversation and put the pâté on his desk. She scooped up some for herself before taking a seat.

"I thought you said it was gross," Kenny said, still looking at the city.

"It's not my favorite, but it's here."

He spun around and looked at her. He had a serious look on his face. She stared back for a moment before continuing to chew.

"If something happens to me, this is all yours."

"The territory?" she said, sounding confused.

"You know that's not an option," he said. "This property. The art collection is important to me, and I know you'll take care of it. Brewster, too."

Brewster looked up and hissed at him.

"Sure, but this place is worth millions."

"Millions of American dollars? So what? This territory is worth more even the richest of humans could fathom."

"I don't know why it matters. You'll live far beyond me."

"Paul's useless and these new idiots sound like they might be a bigger threat than anything I've seen in a while."

"Just livestock, right?"

"Yes, but a lot of humans get killed every year by the beasts they call livestock."

"That's true," she said and looked at the pâté. "Want me to get a train ticket for this morning? Business class on the morning route?"

"No, I want to have a proper breakfast and then get some rest. If I get down there too fast, I'll have to do all of Paul's work. Book me a spot on the evening train. Leaves at 6:00, right?"

"6:30 from Union Station."

"That'll do," he said and looked back at his computer. "I'll have time to slog through the rest of these before heading back upstairs."

"If you don't need anything else, I think I'll get some rest before we go."

"We?" he said and shook his head. "No. You're staying here. Looks like we have eight orders and I need you to make arrangements for more culling visits. I see at least one that wants all vegetarians. I will never understand that."

"That meat is less fatty."

"If you say so," he said, glancing at her. "Go get some sleep after you book my trip. Don't worry about a return ticket. I'll probably be down there for three weeks or so."

"And you don't want to drive?"

"Drive? No thanks. That's boring and I-55 is one of the worst roads I've been on. I'll stick with the train."

"As you wish," she said and left the room.

Kenny rubbed his eyes and looked at the computer again. The smell of the tea caught his attention, so he picked up the cup and took a sip. He thought he would have Marie

package up some to take along. He turned back to look at
the city.

Kenny watched out the window as his train slipped closer to St. Louis. The temperature had dropped during his trip from Chicago, allowing frost crystals to form along the edge of his window. He found those intricate designs interesting and often looked for those naturally occurring patterns in art.

"Mommy! Look!" a young voice said from across the aisle. Kenny glanced at the reflection in the window to see a little girl holding a doll and a winter coat on her lap. Her eyes were wide. "I can't see his reflection."

"Shh, Maya," her mom, Angie, said while scrolling through Instagram. "We'll be off the train in ten minutes."

Kenny turned to look at the girl and winked. She gasped and looked down at her lap. He wore a fedora with a thick overcoat. Most people would be sweating, but he felt comfortable. With fifteen minutes until St. Louis, he decided he would avoid drawing any more attention. He got up from his seat and started back toward the dining car, even though they had stopped service.

He was five feet, seven inches tall, and looked like a typical forty-something businessman, other than his pointed ears, which were tucked into his hat. Some of the Overlords fit the stereotype that the humans had created over the years. Tall, slender figures were common, although only a small portion were what the humans would call white. He had escaped awkward situations because he didn't look the part of what humans were hunting.

There was no need for a suitcase since he kept a full wardrobe at each of his homes. A briefcase with a laptop and a small bag made up his luggage. Both were Italian full-grain leather, since money was not a concern.

"Welcome to St. Louis," said a station employee as everyone filed off the train.

"A pleasure, as always," Kenny said.

He followed the stream of people up the stairs and across the covered bridgeway over the tracks he had just come in on. He glanced west at the half-moon resting just above the skyline.

The crowd reached the main entrance. Some went for the taxi line, others cut off toward the fenced parking lot a half block away, and Kenny went with a group around the corner to the MetroLink station.

He didn't feel like walking all the way home. He knew that if he used his abilities he could run and be there in under five minutes. That always created the risk of being noticed.

He glanced at the schedule displayed near the center of the platform and saw that the next eastbound train would be another eleven minutes. He sighed and pulled his jacket closed.

"Easy target," whispered a man from behind him. Kenny turned to see three men in black coats and jeans walking across the street. They were at least three hundred feet away from him, but excellent hearing was one benefit he had always enjoyed.

He turned further to see the little girl from the train holding hands with her mom. They were approaching the parking lot, but he knew they would have to use a code to get through.

"Her name is Maya," he said to himself and put the strap for his briefcase over his head. As it came to rest on his shoulder, he flexed his free hand. He clipped the small bag in his other hand onto the corner of the briefcase.

"Hey!" called one of the men and the woman turned to look at them.

"Leave us alone," she said, pulling Maya behind her.

"We aren't going to hurt you, but we are going to need your purse," he said. "Tough times, you know."

"I'm just trying to get my daughter home. I don't have any money."

"Well, you probably have a little bit on you. Most people coming in on the train have cash, but we'll settle for some credit cards or medication."

She looked down at the receipt in her right hand. It had 52821 on it, so she reached out to start typing on the keypad to her left. The man pulled a knife from his coat pocket and stepped toward her.

"Stop there," Kenny said, suddenly standing ten feet to the man's left. The woman spun to look at him, too. "Leave her alone."

"Where did you come from?" he said. "This is none of your business."

"Mommy. It's the man from the train," Maya whispered. "The one with no reflection."

"Shh, baby, please don't talk. We'll be okay."

"You boys need to walk back across the street and be on your way," Kenny said.

"A middle-aged pencil pusher thinks he's gonna tell us what to do," he said. He and the others were now facing Kenny. Each held a knife. He noticed they all had a small patch sewn on their coats four inches below the left shoulder blade. "You obviously don't know who we are."

"That is easily one the stupidest things any person has ever said. Nothing good comes after that."

"Look, I'll make you the same offer I made her," the man said, moving his knife to his other hand. "You leave me that briefcase and I'll let you walk away. You look like the type of guy that has insurance on that sort of thing."

"I don't have insurance because I don't need it."

"Look, man," one of the guys said. "You obviously don't get out much or you'd know what these patches mean."

"Fine. I've got some time to listen to your little story but let the lady and her daughter get on home. It's cold out here."

"You're a real smartass, aren't you? Well, no one is going anywhere until we get what we came for! Lady, you set your purse down and then you can go. Dude, you're gonna stick around. We're with the Dracs."

"I've heard of you guys," the woman said. "Here, take my purse. Just don't hurt us."

"Ma'am, keep your purse and you're free to go. Get your daughter home," Kenny said, but she didn't move.

"Look, dude, you aren't in any position to be giving orders. Fact is, we've all got knives, and you have a briefcase."

"I don't need a weapon to take you out. In fact, I was hoping to find some of you posers in the next few days. You saved me some work."

"Kill him," the first guy said.

"Ma'am, please cover your daughter's eyes," Kenny said, and she did. Maya protested for a moment but was unsuccessful in seeing what came next.

Kenny grinned a wicked smile, revealing sharp fangs. That part of the legend was correct. The men paused for half a second before closing in. That was more than enough time for Kenny to handle the situation.

The woman saw little more than a blur, but she heard enough to make her want to puke. The ripping sound of flesh being torn from the bone followed by the splash of blood and other fluids on the pavement overwhelmed her. Her hand started to slip away from Maya's eyes, but the remains of the three men hit the ground before the little girl saw anything.

Kenny picked up the woman and the little girl and rushed them to the other end of the gated lot. He set them down and tore a hole through the chain-link fencing. Both of them felt dizzy, but he waited for them to steady themselves.

"Are you all right?" he asked.

"Did you kill them?"

"Don't worry about them. They won't be bothering you."

"How did you do that?"

"Do what?"

"You moved so fast. I couldn't even see what you did."

"I think you two are very tired," he said. "Please go home and get some rest. Think nothing more about this."

"Not think about it?" she said. Her voice was higher, and the fear was evident. "I was scared of those guys, but you're worse. You're… you're a… a real vampire. But that's impossible."

"Maybe it is, but maybe it isn't. Those guys were just thugs. They won't be bothering you, I promise."

"Because you killed them!"

"Did you see that happen?" he said, still calm.

"No, but we heard it. It was like a lion tearing into a gazelle or something in one of those nature shows. Did you eat them?"

"What? No," he said. "Now, please, go on home."

"Don't hurt us!" she yelled and grabbed Maya again.

"If I wanted to hurt you, I would have done it already. I have been traveling a lot the last few days and would really like to get to my apartment. Have a good night," he said and backed away.

"Can't you just turn into a bat and fly away?" she asked, her voice closer to normal.

"That's not a real thing," he said and smirked. He stopped to grab most of the remains of the three bodies and he was gone. He would send Paul and his men over to clean up the rest of the carnage before dawn.

3

"Closed?" Kenny said, looking at a sign hanging in the window of a coffee and tea shop he enjoyed that had been two blocks from his apartment. "That's disappointing."

"You must be from out of town," said a woman to his right. "They had to shut down about six months ago. Just not enough foot traffic downtown."

"That's too bad."

"Especially since all we have are Dunkin' Donuts and Starbucks now."

"That's even worse."

"Beggars can't be choosers. Right?" she said. "Anyway, the closest Starbucks is around the corner next to the boarded-up remains of Lu's Books. It's been rough down here."

"Sounds like the city needs to find some investors."

"Good luck with that," she said. "Anyway, I gotta get to work."

"Thanks," Kenny said. "Have a good day."

"You, too."

Kenny had a feeling his day wasn't going to be very good, He took out his phone and walked around the corner. The directions the woman had given him were spot on. He paused in front of the former bookstore when he saw that it was for rent. That wasn't terribly unusual for downtown St. Louis but seeing that the building was being offered by Ken McClelland Realty surprised him. He didn't remember buying this one, but it had been a while since he thoroughly went through the financials for his rentals. He took out his phone and clicked on Paul's name.

"Hey, boss man! Are you here? I've been waiting for your call."

"Did you take care of that mess near the train station?"

"Sure. Yeah. I sent two guys over there at four this morning. You told me you'd call first this morning.

"I told you that I'd call you at eight. It's exactly eight."

"Oh, yeah, that's right. So, how's your morning going?"

"Not great. Meet me at the Starbucks near Eighth and Pine."

"I can be there in thirty."

"Fifteen and bring two soldiers with you."

"I can do that if I hurry."

"Good," Kenny said and ended the call.

He slipped the phone back in his pocket and walked to the Starbucks entrance. He glanced through the wide window to see a line of people waiting for their morning fix. A sigh escaped his lips before he went inside.

"Barton? Caramel Frappuccino for Barton."

"Yeah, that's me," said a customer sporting a blue sweater and a man-bun. He squeezed through the small crowd at the pickup counter and took his drink. He made a beeline for the exit.

"Linda? Crème Brulé for Linda."

A short woman in a tan pantsuit bumped into three other customers on her way to the counter.

"Ugh! This has whipped cream. I distinctly said no whipped cream. I want a refund."

"I'm sorry, ma'am. I can remake it," the worker said and reached for the drink.

"Not a chance!" she said and snapped it up. "I want a refund, and I'll take this mistake with me."

"I can't do that."

"Whatever happened to the customer always being right?" she shouted and marched to the door. She bumped into an older, confused couple trying to figure out how to order. "Watch out!"

"Sir? What can I get for you?" a young woman asked. Kenny turned to realize he was next in line but had gotten distracted by the rude woman going out the door. He considered tracking her down.

"Sorry about that," he said. "I'll have tea."

"Sure," she said. "What kind of tea?"

"Earl Grey is fine."

"What size?"

"Hm. I'll take that medium-sized cup."

"The Grande?"

"Is that the medium size?" he asked, pointing at the middle stack of cups.

"Yes, sir. The Grande is sixteen ounces and is our medium-sized drink. Unless you count the Trenta, but that's not available for hot drinks."

Kenny just wanted a cup of tea and knew exactly why he never came to these places.

"Fine, yes. The Grande is perfect."

"Room for milk?"

"No."

"Would you like a scone or maybe a donut?"

"No. Just the tea," he said, pulling out his wallet. He handed her a ten-dollar bill. "Keep the change."

"Oh, but it's only…"

"Just put it in the tip jar," he said and walked away.

He found a booth along the side wall near the back of the store after getting his tea. He waited for it to steep. Even after five minutes, it was weak. He frowned at the taste. He'd have to find a better option in the next few days.

"Hey! Boss Man!" Paul called across the shop. Kenny did not respond. Paul and his men walked over to the booth. "Have you been here long?"

Kenny glanced at his watch and said, "Seventeen minutes. You're late."

"Mr. Grumpy having a bad day?"

Kenny looked up at him and Paul knew he had pushed it too far. He could tell that the boss would be fine with taking his head off at that moment. The other two guys stayed a step behind him.

"Can I grab a coffee before we get started?"

"No. Sit down."

"Right. Okay," Paul said and slid into the bench opposite Kenny.

"You two should sit, too. You look stupid just standing there."

"Yes, sir," the one on the left said and joined Paul.

The second walked to Kenny's side and started to sit.

"Definitely not," he said. "You three can squeeze in over there."

The man just nodded and the other two did their best to make room.

"Now," Kenny said, "let's talk about that Ken McClelland Realty sign I saw out there."

"You like that?"

"Not one bit," he said and took a sip. He shook his head in disapproval. "Gateway Real Estate is the name I authorized in 1973, and it has served me well. What made you think I'd want to change it?"

"I thought you'd like to see your name in print. Show off a little. You know what I mean."

"You make my head hurt, Paul. You know my name isn't really Ken McClelland, right?"

"Well, I mean, that's the name you use."

"Right, but why would I care if it's on a sign? I won't always be Ken McClelland. Probably not more than another decade or two. Then, I have to change everything. It's a real pain and now I'll have to make another business name change."

"I'll handle it," Paul said in a disappointed voice.

"No. Leave it. It's already done. I have a more important task for you. Just don't make any other changes without asking. You're my deputy for this area, for now, so I need you to just take care of day-to-day operations. Nothing more. Nothing less."

"For now?"

"Let's talk about these Dracs. Do we know who is in charge yet?"

"It's only a small street gang," one of the other guys said.

"What's your name?" Kenny asked.

"Craig."

"Shut up, Craig. I am only talking to Paul. You two are here because I have work for all three of you when we're done."

Paul gave Craig a sideways glance with a frown and said, "We don't know who is in charge yet. We've only seen small groups in random places across the city, but they don't seem to be working alone."

"So how do you think we should handle this?"

"I would say we should start wiping them out. I bet that we could take them down in less than a month."

"Slaughter them as a whole? Without being noticed of course?"

"Right. It would have to be done carefully. Cover all the details."

"Like leaving a smear of blood on your cheek?" Kenny asked.

Paul reached out to touch each cheek and saw the blood come away on his fingers. He looked up at Kenny, who was not pleased at all.

"I didn't notice it earlier. Can't look in a mirror, you know."

"Yes, I do know that. Thank you."

"I meant…"

"Please stop talking, you oaf," Kenny said. His voice was low, but stern. He studied each of them for a moment, daring them to speak. "Here's what's going to happen. You're going to scour the city. Take more soldiers with you, if you need them, but never more than three of you together. I want you to track where you see these Dracs."

"Ok," Paul said.

"They've done us the favor of deciding to wear jackets with a logo right on it. That should make the job easy enough, even for the three of you. I want a report in two days of everything inside St. Louis City and County. Try to find out who they are reporting to and where."

"We can do that," Paul said.

"I hope so," Kenny said. "Now, get started."

"Can I get a coffee?"

"By the name of Queen Stephanie herself, if you don't get out of here, I'll kill all three of you right here in front of these people."

The men slid out of the booth as fast as they could, but it was like watching some vaudevillian comedy show. Only Kenny didn't find this one amusing. He noticed a handful of people staring at him after the men scurried out the door.

"I guess I better get moving," he whispered and downed the rest of his tea. He got up, smoothed his shirt, and left without making eye contact with anyone in the shop. He knew he had already drawn too much attention.

He made his way out onto Kiener Plaza, where a light breeze blew in from the west. The Old Courthouse stood four blocks away and he looked from it up to the Arch stretching across the riverfront. He thought back on what the area had looked like when settlers started coming here in the mid-1700s. His relationship with the natives had been good, but he was able to grow and harvest the settlers at a higher rate.

"Are you a Star Trek fan?" asked a kid's voice from Kenny's left.

"I'm sorry?"

"You have pointy ears. My dad likes Star Trek and says the real fans get dressed up as their favorite characters. You must really like Spock."

"Oh, yes," Kenny said, touching the top of his left ear. "Big fan."

"Cool," the boy said and walked away.

Kenny thought back on the years of wearing his hair long and few people even noticed his ears. Things were swinging toward being acceptant of longer hair, so he'd probably grow his back out at some point.

"Where to start?" he asked himself. "Paul and those other idiots better bring some good news. Not going to hold my breath."

The sound of a clip being slid into a gun drew his attention the other way. He couldn't see anyone at first but then found where it was coming from. Two men were on a corner three blocks away under a collection of road signs attached to the upright of the traffic signal. They were talking quietly, and the breeze was just enough to muffle their words.

Kenny squinted at them and saw the Drac patch on each of their jackets. He decided to check them out, so he started walking. They moved out of sight, so he sped up. He raced between two cars waiting to turn left onto Market Street, but they never saw him. He got as close as he wanted just before they stopped outside a small convenience store. The two men nodded to each other, checked their weapons one more time, and then yanked the doors open.

"Everyone get down on the ground! Don't try anything and you'll all be on your way in five minutes!" said one of them as Kenny moved closer. "We are Dracs, and our organization now controls this city. Follow our directions and everyone gets better."

"Take the money!" yelled the manager from the back of the room. "Just don't hurt anyone."

"We want the cash from the store and whatever the customers have on them. We aren't monsters."

"I'd say the opposite," Kenny said. He had come in the door behind them without making a sound. "No one is giving you anything."

Both men spun with their weapons trained on Kenny. He didn't flinch. The customers looked between the three men in a standoff.

"I'd hardly say you are gonna do anything about it," said one Drac.

"He doesn't even have a gun," said the other.

"I don't need a gun for this."

"Sir! Please don't be a hero. Just let them have what they want. I don't want anyone getting hurt. Everyone please get out your cash and give it to them. I can open the safe, but it'll take more than five minutes."

"He's got pointy ears. Shoot him," said the first guy and pulled his trigger. The second guy followed his lead.

They each got six shots off, shattering the pair of glass doors. The customers started screaming, but Kenny wasn't touched. He slid to his left, moving along a row of chips and other snacks. He considered a bag of Cheetos as he came around behind the two Dracs while they took their final shots.

He reached up and grabbed them by their necks. His grip held them steady as they attempted to twist loose. Kenny grinned, thinking he should do this sort of thing more often. Paul would never have messed with this.

"I think two casualties are acceptable," Kenny said and squeezed.

Then, with a vicious twist, he ripped their heads off in a clean motion. Their bodies fell to the ground, with blood spurting from their severed necks.

"Oh my god!" screamed the manager before spraying vomit across the counter.

Kenny dropped their heads and walked to the door. He didn't look back at any of the customers. They would all be in shock long after he left, so he didn't want them to get an extra look at him. The police department would not enjoy this call.

He began to wonder why the first guy had mentioned his pointy ears as he went out the door. The blood on his hands smeared along the handle. He stopped at the curb, thinking he should go home to get cleaned up. His adrenaline was pumping from killing those two, but he knew he had to be careful.

Then, he heard a pop and a short whistle. He felt a sting in his right leg and looked down to see a dart sticking out of his leg. He frowned and reached down for it. The dart was just beyond his fingertips when a powerful dizziness came over him. He tipped to his right and stumbled. He reached for a post to balance himself but missed. Instead, he fell sideways. His head hit the concrete, and he was out.

4

Kenny's head felt like a thick blob of warm pudding when he started to wake up. He couldn't move anything and the sounds around him undulated from near too far. He wanted to open his eyes but only managed the slightest flutter.

"Hey, Rocky. How long do you think it'll take for that dart to wear off?" asked a man with a New Jersey accent. Not a real one, but like a gangster in an old movie.

"I don't know. There was enough in there to take down an elephant."

"Have you done a lot of elephant hunting?"

"Don't be stupid. The boss paid some guy to set up the drugs. He just told me not to touch the tip of the darts."

"Well, I don't trust this guy at all. I saw the mess he made of Russ and Tony back at that store. That was the most disgusting thing I've ever seen! He could be awake right now. Probably waiting for the right moment to rip our heads off, too."

"Okay, Merle. You check the ties then. Those things are supposed to hold a gorilla. Put on four more, if you want."

"I will," he said and picked up the sleeve of thick ties from the table next to him. He pulled four more out and studied them for a minute. Then, he grabbed two more.

Kenny felt a slight tug on his wrists and ankles as Merle put the additional restraints in place. He tried to figure out what had happened but couldn't remember anything after he walked out of the shop. It had clearly been a trap, but how had they known where he would be? The fact that the leader of this group sacrificed two of his own men to set it up made him think that this situation was more dangerous than he thought.

"Satisfied now?" Rocky asked.

"I guess. I might have to add more once we see what he does when he comes around."

"There are six of us. Every super strong person in every movie overpowers groups because they attack one at a time. If this guy tries anything, we rush him as a team. No way he can take us all down. Plus, we have two more darts right here. We'll just drug him again."

"You're way more confident than I am."

Kenny mumbled some nonsense in an attempt to talk.

"See! I told you!" Merle said. "He's awake."

"He can't even move or talk."

"That's what he wants us to think."

"Shut up."

Kenny tried licking his lips. His jaw resisted his attempts to move, and his eyelids felt like they weighed fifty pounds. He sighed.

I gotta get loose and stay away from those darts, Kenny thought. *No shit. Whatever drug they used is really working a number on me.*

"You ready to talk?" Merle asked.

"He can't talk, yet. Besides, we're not in a rush. Get me a beer."

"Get your own damn beer, and I'm not going to be as patient as you. I don't want to die today."

"We're not going to die today. We've been following that Paul guy long enough to know that we've got time to get what we need out of his leader here."

Fucking Paul, Kenny thought.

"Fine," Merle said and walked through the door leading to the kitchen.

"Bring me a Busch Light!" Rocky called after him. "Now, Mr. Kenny McClelland, we have a lot of questions for you, and we know how to make you talk."

Kenny offered no response. He wondered what these guys had in store for him. It sounded like it was going to be a long day.

Merle, Rocky, and the other four guys each finished off a pair of beers before Kenny made any progress toward recovering his senses. Just as Merle smashed a can on his forehead, Kenny blinked.

"There we go," Rocky said. "You can at least blink yes or no to us."

Kenny mumbled something again, but it was nothing more than a babble.

"Let's keep it simple. One blink for yes. Two for no."

Kenny kept his eyes closed at first but then decided to play along for a bit.

"Are you the boss?"

One blink.

"Good. Is your name really Kenny McClelland?"

Two blinks.

"I knew it," Merle said.

"Shut up. I'll handle the questioning," Rocky said. "Now, we know how to neutralize you. Are you willing to concede this area to us?"

Two blinks.

"The Count isn't going to like that."

What a stupid name, Kenny thought.

"Are you a real vampire? Like in the books?"

Three blinks.

"What the hell was that?" Merle asked. "He blinked three times."

"You asked two questions," said one of the other guys.

"What?"

"You asked if he was a vampire and if it was like in the books. He answered both of them."

"Shut up, Kevin."

Kenny gave a short laugh and tried to talk again, but still couldn't quite do it.

"Lift up his head, Merle," Rocky said.

"I don't want to touch him."

"Kevin, you do it."

"I'm not afraid of him or these vampire stories. It's all made up," Kevin said and grabbed Kenny by the hair. He yanked his head up and looked him in the eye. "He's just a guy with some strange ears."

"You," Kenny said.

"Me?" Kevin asked. "What about me?"

"Die," Kenny said, and one corner of his mouth lifted.

Kevin delivered a swift backhand, drawing blood from the corner of his mouth. Drops of crimson smeared across Kenny's teeth and he could taste his own blood. He looked up at Kevin.

"You're not so tough."

"That's enough," Rocky said. He squatted so he could look Kenny in the eyes. "Do you keep your money at your apartment?"

"Some," Kenny said.

"Good. Where's the rest?"

"In… invested," Kenny managed. The slap to the face had gotten his adrenaline pumping. He thought maybe he could push the effects of the drug aside if he tried hard enough.

"That's no good. I bet you have some valuable stuff we can sell."

Kenny just looked at him.

"How many people work for you?"

"None."

"What? We know about Paul."

"Water."

"Answer the question first," Rocky said. "Then, we'll see about a drink."

"No humans," Kenny said, his mouth feeling like cotton. "Just livestock."

"What does that mean?" Merle asked.

"Get him the water," Rocky said.

Kevin went into the kitchen and came back with a plastic cup half full of tap water. He tipped it up so Kenny could get a drink.

"Better?"

"Yes. A little more, please."

Rocky nodded and Kevin gave Kenny a chance at another swallow. He was feeling better.

"What did you mean by 'no humans'?"

"I don't have any humans working for me. You are all livestock to me and my kind."

"Your kind? What does that mean? Vampires aren't people?"

"Definitely not. We were here long before you all were raised up out of the jungle."

"He's making fun of us," Merle said.

"Paul works for you, and he looks just like us. Explain that."

"He's more like me than you. He just doesn't have pointy ears."

"What's with that anyway?" Merle asked.

"Is that really why you all have me tied up? To ask about the genetics of vampires?"

"No, but it's time to get to business. As you might know, we're part of The Dracs. We're taking over St. Louis and the surrounding area."

"That's not going to happen," Kenny said. "Can you let go of my hair? I think I can hold my head up now."

Kevin let go and Kenny's head drooped for a second, but he lifted it back up. He let out a groan as he rocked his head to the right and left. A pop came from the left side. He smiled, revealing his sharp teeth.

"I don't think it's up to you. The Count is going to take you down. He's easily your equal."

"He's not."

"For one, he hires smarter people than you. That Paul guy is an idiot. Anyone could track what he's doing."

"Not going to argue that point."

"Also, the Count looks more like a vampire than you."

"How is that possible?" Kenny asked. "I am a vampire and he's not. Does he wear a cape or something?"

"Here," Rocky said, bringing up a picture on his phone. "That's him."

"He looks more like Count Chocula than Dracula."

"Nope! No way. You don't get to insult him. It's time for your first punishment. Kevin, open the curtains for one second."

Kevin walked over to the window in front of Kenny and flung the curtains open, but quickly yanked them shut. He turned to look at Kenny and then Rocky.

"Well?" Rocky asked.

"Well, what?" Kenny asked.

"Did that hurt?"

"Why would that hurt?"

"Everyone knows that vampires get burned by the sun."

"You said something about Count Chocula hiring smarter people, right? Well, I'll challenge that with the fact that you all captured me in broad daylight."

Rocky stared at him for ten seconds and said, "Didn't think of that."

"What else do you have for me to solve for you?"

"Merle, go get the garlic."

Kenny shook his head.

"No?"

"I mean, I think we can agree that anyone who eats too much garlic is repulsive. I'd definitely move away from them," Kenny said. "And, while we're at it, don't worry about a cross or crucifix. That's nothing to me, either."

"I guess that leaves us with the last weapon in the toolbox."

"Weapon in the… never mind. What is it?" Kenny asked.

"This," Rocky said and picked up a thick, wooden spike from the table behind him. He took a mallet with his other hand. "Don't tell me this doesn't work."

"You finally did it. Drive that stake through my heart and I'm dead."

"Really?"

"Sure, I mean, it's not hard to imagine. Can you think of a living thing that wouldn't die if you put that spike through its heart?"

"He has a point," Kevin said.

"Shut up."

"So, are we done here?" Kenny asked. "The only leverage you have is that stake and killing me means you won't get any answers."

"Let me think."

"Maybe you should call Count Chocula."

"We could kill your sidekick."

"Who? Paul?" Kenny asked. "Don't tease me with a good time. He's the reason I'm here right now."

Kenny twisted his wrists slightly. The feeling was coming back, but he knew he needed more time before he could break free. The zip ties they had used would take him only a second to snap.

"So, what do you guys get out of this? Money? Fame? Fortune?"

"We get to work for the new boss of St. Louis," Merle said. "Too bad you won't be around to see it."

"Right. I'm the Overlord of most of the Midwest, I own a controlling interest in hundreds of businesses that you patronize regularly, and part of an organization that's more powerful than you can imagine."

"The Count is a powerful man," Kevin said.

"He's lunch, if he crosses the wrong Overlord."

"You mean they'd bite him and turn him into a vampire?" Merle asked.

"That's not how it works. It's like saying a human could bite a worm and turn it into a human."

"So, we're like worms to you?" Rocky asked. "Bold statement for a guy we could kill right now, if we wanted to."

"But you won't, because Count Chocula hasn't given the order."

"Stop calling him that."

"No."

"Let's kill him," Merle said. "Then, we can go catch Paul and those other guys. They probably know something."

"Sounds like a solid plan," Kenny said. "He's clearly a better resource than me."

"I tell you what, Mr. Vampire."

"Kenny."

"You turn us into vampires, and we'll help you maintain control of the city."

"I don't need your help. Besides, like I said, I can't turn you into a vampire. It simply isn't something that can be done."

"How do you know?"

"This is boring," Kenny said. He twisted his wrists again and felt the ties dig into his skin. He grinned, knowing he had his strength back.

In a flash, he pulled his arms apart, ripping through the ties with ease. Kevin took a step toward him, but he broke the restraints on his legs with even less effort. He stood and moved past Kevin to the corner of the room. He wanted to get an idea of the challenge ahead of him.

Merle turned to face him and Rocky tapped the mallet to the stake. Kevin pulled out a gun. Kenny assumed it had silver bullets or something stupid like that. The other three guys squared up to him.

"Remember the plan," Rocky said. "All together."

Kenny locked eyes with him and winked.

"Go!"

Kevin was closest, so Kenny went to him first in a blur that the others barely saw. His gun started to come up, but Kenny reached up through his ribcage and tore out his heart in a smooth motion. Before the shock could even register, Kenny threw the heart at one of the other men.

Merle watched as Kevin collapsed to the ground. Then, he heard a gasp and looked up just in time to see the other two guys lose their heads. Panic hit him again and he knew he had been right. He saw the blood drip from Kenny's hands.

"Give up?" Kenny asked. He was staring at Merle, but Rocky was only three feet away. "Too slow."

Kenny rushed forward and grabbed the stake out of Rocky's hand. He spun and drove it through Merle's heart three times. As Merle coughed up blood, Rocky felt a sudden pull, as his body accelerated toward the window. He thought about reaching out for something. But, before his muscles could react, he went through the double pane glass. He was in a slow spin, giving him the chance to look down as he fell three stories to the concrete below.

"I better go get cleaned up," Kenny said with a satisfied grin on his face. "The Count will be sending more guys. I'd hate to be covered in their friends' blood when they get here."

5

Kenny went to the window to look down at Rocky's body. People were gathering around, and one looked up, so he ducked back into the room. The police would arrive soon, so he needed to be long gone. He wiped his hands off on a section of Kevin's clothes that wasn't already covered in blood. He found his briefcase, keys, and other belongings on a side table.

He went through the kitchen and found the back door to the Dracs' apartment. The door led out to a common staircase for five other apartments. It was vacant. Kenny glanced down the stairwell to see where the exit would be. The metal railing was painted lime green with cheap white and gray linoleum tiles. He saw a door leading out onto the main street, which would be too obvious. Then, he saw a ladder leading up to the roof and he decided that would be the better option.

"I hate heights," Kenny said, as he walked across the tarred roof of the building where they had held him. "Not too far to get home, at least."

He stepped across the top of the wall to the next building. The old bricks were in good shape, but he made a note to check out the roofs on his own properties. He continued across two more buildings before reaching the end of the block.

"Being able to turn into a bat and fly home would be nice about now," Kenny said, as he looked down on a side street. "I can't believe I'm doing this."

He made the leap, but immediately felt the pain shoot through his knees. No one noticed the guy coming down from the rooftop. Kenny braced himself against the building

"Getting old sucks. Sucks? Where did that come from?"

Kenny started to his right, thinking that would be his quickest route home. He saw a police car fly past on his left. Rocky's body was almost certainly already on someone's social media feed. That would be a solid distraction to get Kenny back to his apartment.

He walked the next two blocks in something just above a leisurely pace. No one paid attention to him. The desire for a good rest took over his thoughts. He walked up the stairs to his apartment and pulled out his keys.

Kenny picked through them and found the right one. He slipped it in the lock and gave a quick twist, unlocking the door. As he grabbed the knob to open the door, he felt a sharp pain at the base of his neck.

He reached back and touched the spot. Feeling another small dart, he pulled it out and looked at it. Then, he felt the drug kicking in again.

"Damn it."

He dropped the dart and heard footsteps behind him.

"Just relax," said a man's voice from down the hallway. "It's a smaller dose than earlier."

Kenny reached for the wall but could only feel his palm slide along the plaster as he went down. The concrete floor waited as he slumped onto it. His eyes rolled back while he tried to fight off the drug.

"Fentanyl is good stuff," said the voice. "I wanted to keep you from fighting back, but still be able to have a chat."

"What do you want?" Kenny asked, as he fought through a slur of words.

"I have everything I need for now," the voice said. "We'll move forward in a month or so. The problem is that we need to make sure that you're out of the way when I take control."

"You're… the Count?"

"Yes, that's me," the voice said. "I choose to keep a low profile, but we need to make sure we're ready when the time comes. Now, who do you answer to?"

"I'm my own boss."

"I don't believe you. I have two guys tailing Paul, your sidekick."

"I know who he is."

"He'll tell us everything, even if you don't. Kinda looks bad on you to have someone like that as your number one guy."

"Number one in this area. I have other areas."

"Really? Maybe I'll need to expand."

"Never happen. I wasn't ready for you. That's on me," Kenny said before licking his lips. "Anyone who comes after me will be ready to fight."

"I have a lot of Fentanyl and it worked great on you. I'll just use it on them, too."

"Take me inside the apartment."

"What's in there? A trap?"

"No. I just want to get comfortable," Kenny said. "I'm guessing you're going to kill me, so I might as well lay on the couch for a minute."

"You want to die?"

"I didn't say that, but why else would you be here? If this drug wears off, then I'll come for you and all your men."

"We got to you twice. What makes you think the third time would be any different?"

"It just would. I'd be ready. You should see the mess I left at that apartment where you were holding me."

"One of my guys says the cops are already there and the reporters are on the way. Must be gruesome."

"It is. They didn't see it coming."

"Fine," the Count said. "Take him inside."

Two other men came from the shadows and grabbed Kenny under the armpits. They lifted him up and one pushed the door open with his foot. He also shoved the dart away with the tip of his boot, not wanting to risk touching it with his bare hand. That dose only slowed Kenny, but it probably would have killed either of them. They carried him over to a couch covered in gold fabric with burgundy trim.

"That's a fancy couch," the Count said.

"I like it," Kenny said, resting his head back against one of the matching throw pillows. "Try not to mess it up."

"That's up to you. If you can die without bleeding on it, then I'll probably take it back to my place."

"Add thief to your resumé then, I suppose?"

"So do you work for someone or what?"

"I'm in charge of this area. The Council is in charge of everything," Kenny said, feeling very tired. Suddenly, death didn't sound all that bad. "Try not to break too much stuff. Some of it's pretty old. Enjoy whatever you take, but don't say you weren't warned when the Overlords arrive."

"Where's the money?"

"American money? I don't have much here, but the gold is in those vases over by the fireplace. Inconsequential amount compared to what I'm worth and you'll be nothing more than a blood stain on the pavement before long."

"I've done my research, and I know that a wooden stake will kill you," the Count said.

Kenny sighed.

"It would kill you, too."

"You'll never know," the Count said and raised the sharpened wood over his head.

"Fucking Paul."

One of the men who had carried Kenny inside glanced down into a vase near the fireplace. He saw a glint and tipped it to get more light on the gold he saw inside. That triggered an alarm three hundred miles away.

—

Marie was standing in the kitchen of Kenny's Chicago apartment warming up some leftover pizza, when she heard a shrill noise that made her cover her ears. She didn't know what it was, but it was coming from Kenny's office.

She left the pizza and started down the hallway. The desk chair faced out toward Lake Michigan, so she gave it a half turn. Brewster leapt out of her way with a yowl, and she sat down. She typed in the password on the computer and clicked the flashing red box on the bar at the bottom of the screen.

The video came to life, and she saw Kenny stretched out on the couch in his St. Louis apartment. A man was standing next to him with a wooden spike. She heard him say something and then he raised the spike over his head and brought it down as hard as he could.

Marie watched as Kenny lurched when the wood drove through his chest. She didn't know why he didn't fight back but stared in shock as the man with the stake let go and stepped back. He had a grin on his face until Kenny started to convulse. They watched as Kenny relaxed before exploding into a cloud of dust.

The dust settled onto the couch, swirling as it fell. The Count stepped closer to have a look. Marie screamed.

"No! You killed Kenny!"

Marie could only stare as the men started gathering up Kenny's things. She wondered where Paul was and how this was happening. Then, she remembered that he had numbers stored on his desk phone.

The first stored number was listed as Queen and she thought it might be a mistake to call that, even if Kenny had been murdered. The second number said Mother, which seemed like a better option. She picked up the receiver and pressed the button.

"It's been far too long since you called me," said the woman's voice on the other end of the line.

"Um, I'm sorry to bother you," Marie said.

"Who is this?" asked the woman, although her voice remained stoic.

"I'm Marie, Kenny's assistant."

"What has happened to my son? It must be bad if you are calling me."

"I… I don't know how to say this…"

"Is he dead?" the woman asked.

"Um… yes. I just saw it on the surveillance in his St. Louis apartment. It was the most horrific thing I've ever…"

"Let's stop there," the woman said. "I'm his mother and I'll take care of things from here. I know that he wanted you to have all of his possessions in Chicago, so please enjoy them. Especially that art collection. He was very fond of it. Oh, he wanted you to take care of the cat, too."

"Yes, I will."

"Good. I will handle the rest of his business and notify his father. You don't need to do anything else or contact anyone. Please unplug the phone you're using and destroy it, along with Kenny's computer."

"I can do that."

"Good girl. I'll make sure you are all set on money in the next few days, but I need to notify Queen Stephanie. Please do not attempt to call me again. You are relieved of your duties."

"Thank you," Marie said, and the line went dead.

6

Celia hung up the phone and looked across her sitting room. The various marble statues had always made her think of her accomplishments, but suddenly they were unimportant. Her son had been killed and now she wanted revenge, but nothing quick. She wanted a cool, calculated destruction of these beasts that had taken his life.

She glanced over at a picture of a young Hans playing at the base of the Alps with some friend in the snow. She wished she had never let him go to America. Becoming an Overlord had always seemed important, but now it felt insignificant.

He had adopted the name Kenny many years ago, which she hated. He always said it made sense to change his name from time to time to protect his interests. She didn't buy it and had always gone by her true name. Now, she needed to go to St. Louis to find his killers and to take care of the fool, Paul, who she was sure had allowed this to happen.

Celia picked up her cell phone and glanced at the saved contacts. Number one was Steph. She thought about it for a minute and clicked the name of the Queen.

"Hello, My Queen."

"What can I do for you, Celia?"

"My Hans is dead at the hands of some rebellious humans."

"Oh no. We need to send some caretakers in immediately."

"I am confident that his deputy played a role in his death, and I would like to handle that."

"Did he commit treason?"

"I don't think so, but his poor choices certainly led to Hans' death. I can't let that go unpunished."

"So be it. I authorize you to rectify the death of your son, short of imposing a death penalty. Also, the selection of the new owner of the territory must not be affected by your vengeance."

"Yes, My Queen. I will go in and handle my business, but then I will bow out."

"Very well. I will assemble a committee to lead the transition. I'm sorry for your loss."

"Thank you."

—

Celia walked into a conference room two hours later and took her seat. A younger looking woman was at the head of the table. Four others were divided on either side of her. She waited quietly for the meeting to convene.

"Welcome to the committee," said Antonia. "Queen Stephanie chose me to help find the replacement for Kenny in North America's Midwestern Territory. So, we are going to oversee the competition from the Queen's new tower in downtown St. Louis. The Queen has instructed us to relocate to the territory by tomorrow, so that the candidates can begin presenting themselves."

"If I might have a moment of the committee's time before things get started, I would appreciate it," Celia said.

"Very well."

"I have spoken with the Queen, and she has given me authorization to take retribution on my son's former deputy, Paul. He will suffer, but I do not plan to kill him. However, I would suggest that the committee be prepared to replace him."

"The new Overlord will have the freedom to choose their own team, as usual."

"Yes, but I don't think Paul is suitable for the role now and he will likely be useless after I'm done with him."

"Ah," Antonia said. "I understand. What about your son's assistant, Marie?"

"I believe she knew the most of Hans' work and would be a good resource. I am aware that he left her a sizable sum upon his death. She may or may not be interested in continuing in that line of work."

"Anything else?"

"Not at this time," Celia said. "I'll leave you all to your work."

She stood and gave a slight bow to Antonia. Her expressionless face hid the fury she intended to inflict on Paul. Her blood red dress flowed as she slipped quietly to the door and out into the hall.

"Let's return to the business of finding a new Overlord, shall we?" Antonia asked. The others nodded. "The alert has already been sent, so anyone wishing to make a claim and participate in the competition will arrive in St. Louis soon enough."

"Why St. Louis? Chicago was his headquarters," said Einar, a male vampire two seats to her left.

"I believe that the new leader should challenge these humans and destroy them as part of the tests," Antonia said.

"A good point. Please continue," he said.

"We will convene in St. Louis to receive the competitors. Then, we will guide the process. At no time should we intervene. We are there to judge the competition. Nothing more.”

“Understood,” the other four said in unison.

“Excellent. Gather your things for a lengthy stay, although I'm not sure how long this will take. One of the Queen's private jets will be carrying us there. Departure will be in five hours.”

7

Eighteen people gathered in the basement of an abandoned bank in the Tower Grove area of St. Louis. Each wore a vest or jacket with the Dracs patch sewn in the same place near their left shoulder blade. They were spread around the room sipping on beer, soda, or water and having discussions in small groups. A tall, overweight man with closely trimmed hair and a goatee that had recently been dyed black threw open the door and stepped in.

"Attention!" called the big man. He paused to make sure they were listening. "Everyone move to the Count's chamber. He'll be ready in five minutes. Do you have the financials, Lucy?"

"Of course, Helsing," stated a woman standing alone in the back. Her black outfit, makeup, and hair were only broken up by the red patch on her shoulder. She didn't like him and thought his adopted name was a horribly uneducated choice.

"Good," he said. "Oh, Fergus, don't bring your drink in the chamber. If you spill beer on the Count's carpet again, he'll kill you."

Fergus grinned as everyone turned to look at him.

"Seriously. Don't bring it. He'll kill you for real."

"Okay. Okay!" he said and downed the last of his bottle of Modelo. He was soft around the middle and most considered him a bit of a dumbass, but he finished every job the Count sent him on. That earned him a spot in this room.

The group moved toward the door and formed into a line. Helsing led the way and Lucy brought up the end. The short hallway to the Count's chamber was painted black and had only two bare red bulbs for light. The Count thought it set the mood for his work and forbade the use of white lights anywhere except the antechamber where the group had been.

"Don't talk," Helsing said as he slid open the heavy, steel door to the chamber. The red light spilled in, but the darkness swallowed it up immediately. Thirteen blacklights were in sconces around the room. They provided just enough light to allow people to find their seats. The top of each ornate wooden chair bore a number, which had been carefully hand-drawn in paint that would glow in the dark. Each attendee knew which number was theirs. Those with the lower numbers held the most favor with the Count.

Just as the last person settled in, a low tone from an organ started. The minor keys built as they waited. When the music reached its climax and stopped, the Count strode in through an archway at the front of the room. The rustle of his cape was the only sound.

Helsing pushed in the Count's throne-like chair as his leader sat down. The Count looked around the room, studying each face and the different effects the light had on their skin. Finally, he smiled, revealing cosmetically extended canines.

"Friends," he said in a low, powerful voice. "I have brought you here tonight to deliver great news. Through nearly three years of hard work and dedication, we have finally reached our first goal. The city of St. Louis and the surrounding areas belong to us."

He paused, expecting applause. Helsing started clapping and the others followed suit. Once they stopped, he continued.

"We still have much work ahead of us as we grow our enterprise. The people are beginning to fear the Dracs, and that fear will increase as we enter the next phase. We will expand quickly and violently. No one will dare stand up to us. The stories of us killing the old vampire will spread, and the politicians will do our bidding once we start lining their pockets."

"What's our next step?" Fergus asked.

"A fine question. In front of each of you, is an envelope. I don't want you to open them until you are home, and your doors are secured. I have personally written out detailed instructions. In order for us to move to the next level of power, these instructions must be followed with complete precision. You have been assigned a partner in this assignment, which I selected. Two days from now, at exactly nine in the morning, we will make our single biggest move yet. It is critical that you not share your part of the plan with anyone other than those included in your envelope. Any questions?"

"Count," Lucy said. "Our muggings have slowed down a bit and the petty theft isn't bringing in as much cash as it has in the past. What are our plans to bolster the finances?"

The Count smiled, revealing his sharpened canines again.

"That is certainly a valid concern. I believe you will have a better understanding of my cash flow plan after you read what is in your envelope."

"Yes, my lord," she said.

"Very well. I appreciate you all coming here this evening, but I have some matters I must attend to regarding the dead vampire. Enjoy your socializing and I will look forward to seeing you all in two days. I wish you all great success, and you carry my blessing with you."

"Thank you, Count," said the people around the table.

He stood, looked them over, and turned with a swoosh of his cape. Four long strides carried him out of the room. Helsing took his spot standing to the right of the Count's chair.

"Feel free to return to the antechamber for more drinks, but please remember to protect your envelope. There is much to be done before the time mentioned by our lord. Have a good night," he said and lifted his arm toward the exit.

Each of the attendees picked up their envelope and stood. Fergus and two others stopped to have a drink, but the rest left the building. They were eager to see what lay before them in the Count's plan.

8

Maddi Johnson reached into the old Papermill box they used for emptying the night drop every morning at River Bank and Trust. She took a green bank bag and moaned her displeasure when she realized it was for Jerry's Arcade. She would be working through a ton of change and mangled bills for at least an hour. She shook her head and read the number on the lock. She flipped through the keys on a big ring and found the right one. It clicked into place, and she unzipped the bag a second later.

She hated this part of the morning and shuffled her feet as she walked back over to her teller station, knowing they'd be working through these bags until at least eleven. Verifying cash totals and adding up checks was boring, but her job as a whole was less than exciting about ninety-nine percent of the time. She sipped her coffee before pulling out the paperwork.

"Do anything fun last night?" asked Ben Stover from the next teller window. He had the contents of a bag spread out before him.

"On a weeknight?" Maddi asked. "You know better than that. I spent an hour on Netflix and two more on Tik Tok, but nothing fun. You?"

"About the same, I guess. I played Xbox for three or four hours and got a pizza from Imo's."

"Ew."

"Don't judge me, Maddi. It's not like we're getting rich here."

"Fine, but that pizza is gross."

"You have an interesting way of not judging me."

"I was judging the pizza. Not you."

He shook his head without looking up. She laughed. Ben had become a good friend and was one of the few bright spots in her job.

"Time to open the doors," said Linda Jemison, as she walked to the main entrance. "Everyone ready?"

"Looks like we have people lined up out there," said Ben.

"Gonna be one of those days, I guess," Maddi said.

"Fix the attitude," Linda said before unlocking the door. She pushed it open and welcomed the customers in. The first pair came in as she walked back into the lobby. Two others were three steps behind them.

"The Dracs are here!" called out a woman who was second through the door.

The man who had come in first bared his teeth and pulled a pistol from his pocket. He shot Linda in the back of the head, spraying blood across the tan carpet. He knelt down over her, looking for the keys that he knew she would have in her pocket.

"Don't move, don't set off any alarms, and don't be a hero," said the woman. "We're here to rob the bank, but we'll kill you all if necessary."

"What do you want us to do?" Ben asked, putting his hands in the air.

"I want you each to unlock your drawers. I want whoever has access to the main vault to join me with your keys. Do you have the manager's keys, Vincent?"

The man who had shot Linda held up a ring full of keys on an arm band. A smear of blood was turning into a small puddle on the carpet, but only Maddi was watching it spread.

"You two at the drive-through! I want you to pull those canisters in and drop your blinds. The bank is closed. Each of you has exactly one minute to set all the cash from your drawers on the counter. I want the bottom drawers, too. I don't want any dye packs or hundreds that are tucked into alarms. If I see a single cop, we shoot you all. Understood?"

"Yes," Ben said, and Maddi echoed him. The other two tellers agreed as they followed his instructions.

The third person through the door jumped over the counter with a canvas duffle bag and walked back to the drive-through. Those tellers began filling his bag after completing the tasks given by the first Drac.

"You all know who we are, right?"

"Yes," Ben said, taking the lead. "You are the Dracs. We'll do what you want. Just don't hurt us."

"Hurt you? We're here for the money."

"Take it then. Just leave us alo…" Ben said but was cut off as the Drac who had gone to the drive-through jumped on his back and drove a dagger into his neck.

They collapsed to the ground and the Drac bit into his throat with a primal yell. Maddi flattened herself against the wall and put her hand over her mouth, trying to hold in a scream. The last Drac grabbed the bag of cash on her station but made no other moves toward her.

"Let's go!" called the first Drac and they all moved toward the main entrance. The one that had stabbed Ben looked up with a disappointed look on his face. He had blood smeared around his mouth. He pulled the blade out and lapped at the flow of fresh blood. Maddi stared in disbelief, trying not to vomit.

An hour later, one of the local news stations was set up and ready to report on the robbery. A young woman in a purple and white dress took her place at the edge of the bank parking lot. The breeze blew on the hem of her dress, on what should have been a beautiful day in the city.

"This is Marilyn Meyers with KMOV news. I am reporting from the River Bank and Trust branch at Vandeventer and Chouteau. This is one of the nine banks in the last hour to report a robbery. It seems that an organized attack on these banks was put in place this morning. There have been no less than twenty-five casualties across the affected banks. A disturbing scene as many of the victims have been bitten on the neck in a vicious manner. Witnesses say that perhaps they even had their blood sucked in a vampire-type attack. What we do know is that each branch has a large, red, spray-painted Dracs logo in the center of the lobby floor. Survivors of the robberies have made statements that the thieves claimed to be with this new organized crime regime. Police have not issued a statement yet. If you have any tips on these crimes, please contact the St Louis City Police. Stay safe."

9

The double doors slid open, allowing Celia to stroll into the Four Seasons hotel in St. Louis. A bellhop was close behind with her luggage. She took a good look around, judging the decor and cleanliness of the lobby. She thought it was better than expected, but the hotels and buildings in the Americas would never measure up to those at home. The sooner she could clean up the mess with Hans, the sooner she would be able to go back to her estate in the Alps.

"Welcome, Ms. Celia Jones," said the attendant at the front desk. "We're glad to have you joining us this evening. Your travel agent completed all your paperwork ahead of time, so you're all set on that end."

"Yes," Celia said. "I'm pleased to be here. What is my room number?"

"You will be in room 513."

"Fine, fine," she said, looking at the attendant's empty hands. "Can you make two keys for my room?"

"Anything for a platinum-level guest," he said. "Give me just a moment and I'll have you all taken care of."

A minute later he handed her a pair of key cards and smiled. She nodded and took the paper folder with both keys.

"Wi-Fi is complimentary for platinum guests and your password is printed on the inside of the key folder."

"Thank you," she said, without looking at the password. She never used Wi-Fi and didn't trust its security. The Overlords had their own satellite network, and she would connect to the internet directly through that.

"Barry will take your bags to your room for you," he said, gesturing toward the bellhop.

"Yes. Will you please add a twenty dollar tip for him to my bill?"

"Happy to do that for you."

"Good," she said and turned for the elevators. She wanted to get down to business but was careful to avoid drawing attention from any petty humans. Demolishing the lot of them in the wake of her current plan would be reasonable in her mind.

Barry stood against one side of the elevator as they went up. His knuckles were white, as he gripped the brass bars of the luggage cart. When they had stepped into the confined space a puff of air had come from the elevator shaft, tousling her hair and revealing one pointed ear.

Once in her room, she pulled a laptop from her briefcase and put it on the mahogany table near the window. She did not open the curtains. The suitcase she had brought along stood idly by, waiting for attention. Instead, she drew a phone from her inside coat pocket and dialed.

"Celia," said the man's voice on the other end of the call.

"What time is the meeting?"

"I have a room reserved at a steakhouse downtown at eight. I'll text you the location."

"You know I don't eat beef."

"It is an Overlord-friendly steakhouse."

"And the meal?"

"Salad, bread, and some special Cajun cuts brought in from Louisiana."

"Cajun," she said. "Sounds nice. It has been many years since I had that."

"Very well. See you soon."

She tapped the end button and set about unpacking. Seven outfits made up the entirety of what she had brought along, but she had no plans on staying for a full week. She certainly had no interest in being part of finding Hans' replacement.

—

Downtown St. Louis was a hodgepodge of buildings. Some had sprung up in the last twenty years, while obnoxious ones hailed from the 1960s and 70s. Celia didn't recognize any of them but was happy to see some of the hundred-plus-year-old buildings in the blocks north of Busch Stadium. Baseball was a sport she never could grasp. Hans had loved it for some reason.

The steakhouse, Barlow's Eatery, occupied part of the first floor of what had once been the Midwestern Mercantile Building. Five small shops faced the street, and Celia had to check the directions again to locate an open-air corridor between two of the shops that led to four others toward the back. The rear spots were not great for drawing in foot traffic, but those shops looked like they had been there a long time.

"Cajun," she said quietly, as she opened the door to the restaurant.

A man in a tuxedo stood at the host stand. He offered a well-practiced smile as the door closed behind her and said, "Good evening. Do you have a reservation with us tonight?"

"I'm joining Russell's group. Probably in a private room."

"Ah, you must be Celia?"

"I am."

"Yes, Russell let me know you'd be arriving soon," he said and raised his left hand toward the bar area. A young woman walked over to join them. "Please take our guest to the Stoker room."

"Cute," Celia said.

"Yes, ma'am," he said and swept his right hand toward a hallway in the opposite direction from the bar. "Have a good evening."

The young woman led her along the hallway to the last door on the right. Celia could tell she was a commoner, but that was still much better than being served by a human. The woman gave a quick tap on the door and waited for acknowledgement.

"Come in!"

The woman pushed the door open without going inside. Celia nodded as she moved past her and approached the center table. The three people at the table stood up. The woman closed the door.

"Welcome, Celia," the man on the far side of the square table said. "I'm Russell."

"Very good," she said, still standing next to her chair. She looked at each of them, waiting for one of them to act. Suddenly, the man to her right stepped over and pulled out her chair. She sat.

"Please sit," she said, once her chair was comfortably in place. "I'm looking forward to this meal you spoke of, but I'd like to get some formalities out of the way first. Names?"

"Yes, I'm Russell, we spoke on the phone. I've brought along Carmen and Anmol. We all worked for your son through Paul. Might I say that we are very sorry for your loss?"

"Thank you, but let's stay focused on the task we are here to address. I will mourn my son soon enough. What are your roles in this district?"

Russell said, "I'm an accountant of sorts. Not a big fan of the rougher side of our work, but processing the money is something I've gotten quite good at."

"Not a big fan of what exactly? You don't approve of the meat processing? Perhaps the enforcement of our rules?"

"Oh, no, I meant I prefer not to participate in it. I have no soft place for humans."

"Fine. What about you, Anmol?"

"I'm what many call a software developer. That's a bit of an oversimplification. We have some extremely complex software running behind most of what we do. I've been at this for decades and love staying on the cutting edge of anything new. Part of my duties include hacking into new human databases to gather information."

"That could prove useful. Carmen?"

"Personnel. I know everyone who works in the district, how long they've been here, and what they do."

"Excellent," Celia said. "Why are the three of you coming forward to assist me? This could be viewed as insubordination or even treason."

"We discussed it after Kenny's death," Russell said. "The fact is that we hope that whatever brought about his death was not treason because we are eager to get a new

Overlord installed. Treason would lead to a drawn out investigation and a lag in direction for the territory. However, we have no respect for Paul. He has led this city poorly, to say the least. If Kenny had a normal sized territory, instead of one of the old ones, he would never have left Paul in this role. There were rumors that he was here to replace Paul when he died."

"Perhaps he was, but that is unknown. So far, we are leaning away from treason," Celia said. "Carmen, do you know where Paul is now?"

"Unfortunately, not. I know where he should be, but he dropped off the grid within an hour of Kenny's death."

"Will operations continue without his participation?"

Russell said, "To be honest, we've operated without his involvement for quite a while. His decision making skills are, how should I say, not good. An email was sent to the entire St. Louis organization from Kenny the morning after he arrived. He told us not to process any further legal documents without his personal approval."

"One of my contacts said that Kenny was upset with Paul setting up new corporations and changing names without consulting him," Carmen said. "He never looked more than a year down the road when doing anything, really."

"And his finances?"

"Paul's? Well, he's been around for a long time and held the top spot for as long as any of us can remember. I would assume he has a nice nest egg," Russell said.

"He is doing quite well," Anmol said. "Kenny kept tabs on his team's finances, although not everyone knew it. My team of hackers has access to all banking records of every employee."

"Really?" Carmen asked.

"Don't overthink it. We're not changing anything."

"Still, it would have been nice to know."

"Back to the topic, please," Celia said. "If Paul were to withdraw money from any of his accounts, would you be able to locate where it happened?"

"Sure. Within seconds."

"Good, here is my number," she said, handing him a plain white business card with a phone number and nothing else printed on it. "I want you to watch anything he has access to and set an alert for any activity. Text me with instances that may be one of his known close associates and not him but call me immediately if something happens that indicates his location."

"What would you like us to do?" Russell said, gesturing toward Carmen.

Celia gave them each a card and said, "Same instructions for the two of you. If you hear a rumor or get any kind of communication regarding Paul, you let me know. I'll be doing my own research."

"It's likely that he has quite a bit of cash in physical form. Gold or cash in the thousands are not uncommon for those at his level."

"Thousands?"

"Maybe ten to twenty, I suppose," Russell said. "That could sustain him for a while."

"My son kept significantly more than that in each of his apartments, so why wouldn't Paul have more?"

"He might have," Carmen said, "but I don't think he would be smart enough to plan ahead. He honestly believed he was on good terms with Kenny."

Celia nodded her understanding. They were all watching her when another knock came at the door. It swung open and a woman in a pristine white outfit came through, pushing a cart. She stopped between Carmen and Celia.

"Dinner is served," she said and removed the silver covers from two of the plates. "Blue rare Cajun filets with twice baked potatoes and grilled asparagus."

"Very nice," Russell said as the server placed the dishes in front of the ladies. She then continued to the direct opposite corner to serve him and Anmol. "Please add the entire meal to my tab."

"That won't be necessary," Celia said and produced seven crisp folded one hundred dollar bills from a pouch in her pocket. "I appreciate the help you are all offering, so I'll buy dinner. Further rewards will come with more information. Will this cover it?"

The server glanced at the money and looked surprised.

"This is far more than the bill for this evening. I'll get you some change, ma'am."

"I do not require change. Keep that for yourself. Discretion is important, and hopefully that will make sure you forget we were here. If there are any records of the reservation, make those go away."

"As you wish," the server said and went to the door, pulling it closed behind her.

“Bon appétit,” Carmen said and slipped her knife into the meat. The red juices flowed out onto her bone white plate.

10

In the early 1900s, an architect named William B. Ittner designed hundreds of school buildings throughout the state of Missouri. Almost fifty of those were built within the city of St. Louis. They had beautiful hardwood floors, tall windows, and plenty of room for students to learn.

As the decades slipped past, white flight and reduced education budgets allowed the buildings to fall into disrepair. Eventually, with a drastically reduced population, the city began combining the schools and then replacing them with more modern structures. The beautiful old buildings were either demolished or sold off to private investors.

One that was sold off was a middle school in the south part of the city. It had three stories and had been one of the last few used by the district. Sometime in the 1980s, a multipurpose addition had been built onto the rear of the building to be used as a gymnasium and lunch room. The developer was turning the classrooms into condos and didn't have much of a use for the addition. He went with easy money instead, choosing to lease it out long-term for five thousand a month to an individual who stated he would be using it for storage.

That individual was Connor Lewis, but he leased the space under his assumed name of Louis Rogers. He came from a white middle-class family and had attended the University of Missouri before starting his career in banking with River Bank and Trust. At his ten-year mark in the industry, he was promoted to branch manager, which allowed him to sit in on more important and informative meetings.

Bank vice presidents often used those meetings to talk about major investors in and around the city. All branch managers had been made aware that anyone representing Gateway Real Estate should be given priority attention over everyone else, including the Busch family. Connor started researching this real estate company.

After a year, he started recruiting low-level criminals to work for him. They would do carjackings, muggings, theft, and robberies. He gave generous cuts to his people to develop loyalty. They brought in friends and the group thrived.

Finally, Connor learned about Kenny McClelland due to some sloppy paperwork filed in the circuit court by one of Kenny's assistants. He would learn that many people believed Kenny was a vampire, like those in the storybooks. This led Connor to choose the name Dracs for his crime syndicate. It caught on quickly and people treated his people differently with this new belief, while he continued his day-to-day work at the bank. None of his people knew his real name, but they came to call him the Count.

"What time is this thing supposed to start?" asked a woman standing along the back wall of the former gymnasium.

"Who cares?" said a man to her left. "The Count will be here when he gets here. You got somewhere to be?"

"I asked a simple question," she said, baring her teeth at him.

"Both of you need to shut the fuck up. The Count will start the meeting when he is ready."

"Who the hell are you to be giving orders?" the man asked.

"I'm Lucy."

"So?"

"Shut up, Jack," another guy said. "She's one of the inner crew."

"Oh."

"Good," Lucy said. "We all work toward the same goal here and you're going to like what's coming tonight."

"What is it?" Jack asked.

"Dude."

"All right. All right,"

Lucy moved off around the room, listening to conversations and making sure everything was ready. Most of the others from the inner crew were doing the same thing. Only Helsing was with the Count.

"Sir," Helsing said, making his way into the room that had once been the P.E. teacher's office. The walls and floor were painted solid tricorn black, and a single black, wooden desk stood in the center of the room with a dozen small candles burning on it. "Things are almost ready."

The Count turned in his black, leather chair. He had his hands steepled together, with the tips of his index fingers touching his lips. His eyes studied the flickering flames.

"Thank you, Helsing," he said in a low, calm voice. "I know we have many new members here tonight. Any security risks?"

"None so far. Edward and Jasper did a thorough search of the building early today and have been checking everyone coming in."

"Good. Give them my thanks."

"I'm not a fan of their choice of code name."

"It is irrelevant," the Count said, looking up at him. "Each member of the inner circle is allowed to choose their own name, just as you chose Helsing."

"But my name is in Dracula, not Twilight."

"Have you read the book?"

"Well, no."

"Try it sometime. The fact that you use Helsing and I still keep you in this role should be evidence enough that the names are irrelevant."

"I'll get a copy tomorrow, sir."

"Good. Go tell them to get everyone seated and bring down the lights. I want the fog machines on with the red back lights tonight. This is an important evening."

"We'll be ready in five minutes."

"Thank you, Helsing."

Helsing went out, closing the door behind him. He walked along a short hallway that was also painted black. He stopped at a metal door and swung it open six inches.

"Bram, let everyone know that we are about to start, and they should take their seats. Let Lucy handle any issues. I'm about to take down the lights."

"Very good, sir," Bram said, walking away to find Lucy.

Helsing continued along the hall and up a half-flight of stairs. The last door opened into a control room at the back of the stage. He powered up the sound system and activated the fog machines. The house lights came down as people moved toward rows of metal folding chairs and bleachers. Red light came to life at the back of the stage, illuminating the growing clouds of fog.

As soon as he had everything set, he went back to the hallway. The Count was standing at the entrance to the stage, looking out into the darkened room.

"Good to go, sir."

The Count nodded and two bulky men pushed him out onto the stage on a golden throne situated on a rolling platform. Everyone in the room jumped to their feet and began applauding. Shouts of praise echoed in the darkness. He took it all in with only a simple smile and a nod.

"Dracs!" he shouted, after waiting a minute. "Please take your seats!"

The applause and cheers came to an abrupt halt. The only sound was chairs scooting as people sat. He held his arms up and to the side in a welcoming gesture.

"Welcome!" he said, looking out into the crowd. His hair was slicked back perfectly. He had shaved only an hour before and put on a black wig. His assistant had applied a layer of white face paint, black eyeliner, and red lipstick. The tips of his cape were connected to the ends of his tuxedo coat sleeves, creating the perfect persona for the Count. "Tonight is a momentous evening for all of us. Even those of you who have recently joined us will enjoy the prosperity that is soon to come!

"Less than a week ago, some of my most trusted soldiers pulled off the biggest act of organized crime this city has ever seen. I could not be prouder of these people and what they did for us all. The name Dracs is now on the lips of every man and woman in the area. They fear us and are learning to stay out of our way. The bank heist I orchestrated resulted in an influx of funding that was double what I had expected. As usual, those involved have been rewarded.

More of you will be taking part in these big events in the coming months and years. You, too, will have more money than you've ever had.

"All I ask of you is complete loyalty and trust in me. I will lead you to great heights. But anyone who disappoints me or crosses me will be taken care of. The Dracs do not have time for traitors or anyone wishing to act on their own accord. Follow my lead and you will advance in this organization. My inner circle will grow, and the next addition could be any of you. The things you do for me will be the sole factor in that advancement.

"Now, we move to the biggest announcement of the evening. There is another supposed crime organization that has been operating in St. Louis for many years. However, you will all be pleased to know that my inner circle and I worked tirelessly to track down their leader. I killed him with my own hands!"

The crowd cheered and the clapping pleased the Count. He allowed it to naturally die down before continuing.

"Yes! I killed him and not one attempt from his organization has been made to exact revenge. Can you imagine someone thinking they are in charge of a group and no one under them, not one person, has tried to come after us.

"I know that, if my reign were to come to an end at the hands of an enemy, each one of you would attempt to bring vengeance upon them. That is why I am proud to stand here this evening and announce that we have won! We are the victors and now control the city of St. Louis!"

Everyone rose and started yelling their praise. A chant began to build through the noise, and the Count welcomed it.

"Long live the Count! Long live the Count!"

He let it continue for a minute and then raised his hands to call for silence. The noise did not fall away quickly, but they did as he wished over the next few moments.

"I appreciate each one of you and look forward to the next time we gather together. Until then, I will keep working hard, as I know you will. Tonight, I must go on to take care of further preparations. You all are welcome to stay here and celebrate. The bar will open at the back of the room in five minutes, and everything is complimentary this evening! Thank you again and enjoy!"

Helsing pressed play on his computer and turned the volume up. The thud of heavy dance music filled the room as the Count made his exit. Once Helsing knew he was back to his office, he turned the house light up halfway. The party was underway.

A small group of smokers stood outside the Enterprise Center in a fenced-in area sectioned off for those needing a fix during the hockey game.

"Ready to go back in?" asked one woman to another.

"Yeah. I should've worn my jacket."

"Me, too," the first one said and dropped her cigarette butt into a silver can with some sand in the bottom of it. "Intermission's probably over."

The second nodded and walked to the door. She pulled it open and waited. Two other people started in with them. A man in a black hoodie with dark blue jeans and a gray backpack walked by on the opposite side of the road. No one paid attention to him.

He continued down two more blocks to the Union Station parking lot. It was close to full capacity, thanks to the game. The lot attendant sat in the tiny booth reading a book. She didn't notice the man walk by.

Winding through the cars, he made his way to the back section of the lot, which held fifty to sixty vehicles. There he saw his selection for the night. It was a later addition to the lot and couldn't be seen from the attendant's booth. It was tucked neatly up against the interstate right-of-way.

"That'll do," he said, eyeing a lifted Chevy truck sitting in the back row. It was backed in and the driver had straddled the line to secure two spots for his display of insecurity. That allowed the man more space to work.

He went to the darker side of the truck and swung his backpack off his shoulders. He had a laptop and a pair of small devices that would let him access the truck's computer system. He started typing away.

Two minutes later, there was a double click sound and the doors were unlocked. The vehicle thought he was using the remote, so the alarm was deactivated. He quickly bagged up his gear and walked around to the driver's door.

He pulled out on the handle, and it opened. The man smiled, knowing this would be a big score. That's when he noticed a shadow on the pavement next to him. He turned to see a silhouette in the bright parking lot lights.

"Hey," he said.

"Hey, yourself," the silhouetted man said.

"Can I help you?"

"I think so."

"What does that mean?"

"I think you can help me."

"Uh, I think I'm just gonna get out of here," the man said and started to get in the truck.

"No, that will not work for me," the figure said.

As the thief's foot touched the chrome running board, he felt a strong hand on his shoulder. The next instant, he found himself on the pavement, his head radiating pain from the spot that had hit the ground.

"What the fuck, man?"

"I cannot let you steal this truck."

"It's my truck," the thief said, trying to sit up.

The figure turned to look down at him. The thief could see his fangs and the tips of his ears poking through his thick blonde hair.

"Look. Hey. I've heard about you guys. I'm not hurting anyone. This guy probably has insurance."

"You've heard of us?"

"Yeah, the Dracs. Robbed those banks and stuff," he said, starting to scoot away. "You can have the truck. Just let me go."

"I'm not with these fools you call Dracs. They are pitiful humans who wish to be more than they ever will be."

"Then, you're real?"

"Quite."

"Look. Seriously. Just let me go and you can have it. That thing has to be worth sixty thousand!"

"I don't need the money. I need to make a statement."

"A statement? What does that mean?"

"The Dracs think they are in charge, but they aren't. Not even close."

"Okay, man. That's cool. I believe you."

"Good. Now THEY need to believe," he said and dropped to a knee next to the thief. The corners of his mouth turned up with malintent. The thief peed himself. "This is going to hurt."

"No!" the thief screamed as the fanged figure placed the tips of his rigid fingers against his gut.

He pressed and spread his fingers apart, ripping open the shirt and the skin beneath. The thief threw back his head and started slapping at the penetrating hand. It was useless. Blood ran out of the widening gash as the thief's body spasmed.

"That's enough suffering," the figure said and collapsed the thief's head with a single punch.

He proceeded to withdraw the thief's small intestines and arrange them in a large circle on the light gray pavement, which started turning black. He dipped his hand into the open wound and covered his fingers in blood, like a quill in an ink pot.

He wrote 'DRACS' in big letters inside the circle of intestines. After a moment to appreciate his work, he used a straightened section of intestines to bisect the circle. He wiped his hand on the thief's pants and stood up.

"That should get the point across."

The thief's phone dinged. The fanged man pulled it from the right front pocket of his jeans. There was a text.

'Where are you????' was the text on the screen. The figure looked at the fingerprint access on the screen and then down at the thief. He grabbed the man's right thumb and tore it off. He wiped off the blood and pressed it to the screen. It unlocked.

'I got the truck'

'Should have been here ten minutes ago'

'I forgot the address'

'Damn it, Frenchy. You're almost useless. Scroll up.'

The figure did just that and saw the location.

'Got it'

'Well hurry the fuck up. Boss will be here soon.'

'On my way'

The figure brought up Google Maps on the phone and put in the address.

"Three miles," he said.

He dialed 911.

"911. What's your emergency?"

He dropped the phone on the body, turned to his left, and raced out across the interstate toward the address. The handful of drivers on the highway might have caught a blur as he went by.

He came to a stop seconds later next to a large oak tree across the street from a concrete block building. It had been painted white at some point, but large pieces of the old lead paint had flaked off. The windows had flattened cardboard moving boxes taped to the inside.

A late model Mercedes C-Class slowed as it approached the roll up door on the block building. There was a pop and the squeal of metal wheels as the door slowly rose. When it was about a foot above the roof of the car, it stopped. The car went in. The figure rushed in behind it. Neither the driver nor the man running the door saw him.

"Hi, Boss," the man at the door controls said when the driver got out. He wore a black polo with black jeans. Brand new Jordans completed the look of a west county white guy that had no business in that old shop. He pushed the down button to close the door.

"Where's the truck, Doug?" asked the boss. He was a short, chubby man in a custom gray suit accented by a red tie. His frown looked permanent. His thin, stringy hair was plastered to his liver spotted scalp.

"He should be here any minute."

"You said he'd be here before me. You said he was quick. Is this what I get for letting you hire your own person?"

"No. He sent me a text five minutes ago. Might have had trouble getting it out of the lot or something."

"You've got five more minutes. Then, your cut starts dropping."

"Okay," Doug said. He grabbed his phone and tapped Frenchy's name. "Pick up, asshole."

There was half a ring and then his voicemail picked up. Doug hit end and started toward the regular door to look outside.

"He's not coming," the figure said from the back of the building, stepping into the light.

"Who the fuck are you?" Doug asked, pulling a small pistol from his pocket.

"What is this, Doug? You gave someone the address?"

"No. I mean, I told Frenchy, but that's it," he said and pointed the gun at the figure. He noticed the pointy ear sticking out of his hair on the left side of his head. "I asked you a question!"

"Well, you didn't ask it in a very polite way."

"Answer me or I'll shoot."

"Jaroslaw."

"That's your name?"

"Yes."

"Bullshit," the boss said. "Shoot him."

"You're a rude little man," Jaroslaw said. "How do you sell the cars you steal?"

"I told you to shoot him!"

Doug pulled the trigger. The bullet ricocheted off the back concrete wall and lodged in a wooden post holding up a staircase. A second later, his hand and the gun were torn from the end of his arm. Blood spurted out of the fresh wound. Doug grabbed at it with his other hand and turned to his boss in total shock.

"Now," Jaroslaw said, "how do you sell the cars you steal?"

"Fuck you," the boss said.

"That's no good," Jaroslaw said and caved in the top of his skull with the gun he had taken from Doug. The boss's knees gave out first. Then, he tipped sideways onto the concrete floor. Jaroslaw looked back to Doug. "Do you want to bleed out?"

"I…"

"Okay," I'll leave you to it.

He went to the controls and opened the overhead door. Someone would notice the dead bodies before long. That would be good enough.

"Oh, wait," he said and went back to Doug. He grabbed his bleeding arm and pulled him to the ground. He drew a circle with a line through it and added the word 'Dracs' to the middle. Doug tried to stay upright on his knees but ended up on his face at the edge of the circle.

Jaroslaw was satisfied with the message, so he walked outside. He took a deep breath and looked both ways, wondering what to do next. The instructions to make his claim were vague.

"Greetings," said a woman from his left. He hadn't noticed her.

"Oh," he said, taking a step back. "You are?"

"I am Antonia. I'm the head of the committee sent to monitor the competition to decide the next Overlord for this territory."

"How did you find me?"

"You can't be serious," she said, studying his eyes. "You are serious. How disappointing. You went stomping around the city, causing a ruckus. How could we not notice you?"

"Stomping around the city?"

"Don't worry about it. We have work to do."

"What do you want me to do?"

"The Council owns the penthouse apartment at One Cardinal Way," said Antonia. "I want you to report there at ten in the morning. Please don't do anything else between now and then. Your claim is duly noted."

"How many others are there?"

"You are the first, but there will be others."

"How do you know?"

"There are always others. This territory is too large to go unchallenged."

"I see."

"I highly recommend that you not use any of your superhuman powers until tomorrow. Do not draw any extra attention."

"I can do that."

"Good. The committee will be waiting for you."

"Thank you," he said.

Antonia nodded and disappeared. Jaroslaw thought she went back toward the interstate but wasn't completely sure. She was much faster than him. He hoped no one like her would be joining the competition.

12

Chuck's Corner Market occupied the bottom floor of a three-story brick building in the north part of the city. There were signs glowing in the window promoting Budweiser, the Missouri Lottery, Swisher Sweets, and food specials. It wasn't a large space, but it was the only option for basic groceries for over a mile in any direction. Chuck and his family stayed busy from morning to night.

"Hey, Chuck," said a tall, black man in a plain green t-shirt and blue jeans.

"Hey, Stretch," Chuck said, without looking up from his paperwork.

"Can I get a pack of Reds and a lighter?"

"Sure," Chuck said. He was a small man with wispy gray hair that stood in contrast to his dark skin. He wore one of his many pressed white shirts that served as his uniform, something he swore he would never give up. He got the cigarettes and gestured to the small rack of Bic lighters. "Take your pick. It's ten bucks including tax."

Stretch pulled a roll of bills from his pocket and picked out a ten. He put it on the counter, took his cigarettes, and selected a lighter with an American flag on it.

"That's funny," he said, looking at the lighter.

"Yeah. They sent me a variety box."

"Hey, Frank said he might need to use the store room in a little while."

"We're doing stocking tonight," Chuck said, returning to his paperwork.

"All right, old man," Stretch said and put a hundred on the counter. "Thought maybe you'd go easy on me tonight."

"It's not personal, Stretch. I got bills to pay."

"I get it. Frank will be here in less than ten minutes. Probably only need it for half an hour."

"That'll be fine. Let me know when you're done, so I can send my grandson back there to get his work done."

"Will do," Stretch said. He tapped the pack against his hand and then pulled the ribbon that released the wrapper. He took out a cigarette and placed it on his bottom lip. He flicked the lighter.

"Outside."

"Yes, sir," Stretch said, a smile playing across his face. "Always a stickler for the rules, Chuck."

"Mmhmm."

Stretch walked outside and lit the cigarette. There were three other men sitting around a black metal patio table playing dominoes. They each had a beer and their own cigarettes.

"Your turn, Stretch," said the man in the chair opposite the empty one that Stretch had been using.

"Frank's almost here," he said, looking at his watch.

"If you were winning, you wouldn't be holding things up."

"That's not what I'm doing, Shade, and you know it."

"Bullshit."

"Eat a dick," he said. He looked along the street to his left, took a deep drag, and blew out a thick cloud of smoke. A silver Lincoln approached at a crawl. "There he is."

"Damn it," Shade said. "Now you'll never finish this."

Stretch took another drag and dropped the remaining half of the cigarette to the sidewalk. He crushed it out with the toe of his brown leather dress shoe before walking to the curb to greet Frank.

"Hi, boss," he said after opening the back passenger side door. "The back room is ready for you."

"Thanks, Stretch," Frank said as he stood up. His suit was perfect, but he took a minute to brush off imaginary lint. He was barely five and a half feet tall, but the wrinkles around his eyes plus the thick scar on his left cheek showed he had fought a long time to get where he was. He looked over at the dominoes table. "You all just gonna sit there?"

Shade and the others jumped up and made their way toward Frank.

"A little respect goes a long way," Frank said. "You all forget who pays you?"

"No, sir," Shade said.

"Clarence," Frank said to the driver, "go park this thing somewhere else for a bit. I'll call you when I'm ready."

"Yes, sir," Clarence said. When Stretch closed the door, the car pulled away at the same crawl.

"Let's get down to it, Stretch," Frank said. "Barney, you come back with us. Shade and Knuckles, you two make sure we aren't disturbed. Got it?"

"Yes, sir," Shade said and motioned for Knuckles to go back to the table with him.

Stretch led the way to the store and opened the door for Frank. They went in and continued straight back to the store room. Chuck didn't look up. He and Frank had agreed years ago not to do business one on one. It gave Chuck a potential out if things went sideways. Barney, Stretch, and Frank went through the swinging stainless steel door at the back of the store.

"All right," Frank said. "How much heroin do we have stashed here?"

"About three weeks' worth," Stretch said.

"Weed?"

"Maybe two weeks," Barney said. "The school scene is going well this year. That stuff is flowing like water."

"Okay," Frank said. "Keep the heroin off their grounds. Our boys will be in deep shit if they get caught with it there. Weed can be figured out. How many boys do we have right now?"

"Seventeen at the moment," Stretch said, "but I've got two more potentials on my agenda this week."

"Don't get greedy. Cap it at twenty. We want to cover the area, but I don't want them fighting with each other to make quota."

"Yes, sir."

"What do you two have for me before we get to my big topic?" Frank asked.

About that time a man in a dark green hoodie with tan jeans walked toward the store. He had a brown backpack over his shoulder. He paused and looked at the men at the dominoes table.

"You need to keep moving. Either get in there, buy what you need and leave, or just leave," Shade said.

The man studied him for a moment longer.

"You deaf?"

"No."

"Then, you best make a decision really quick," he said, pulling back his jacket to reveal the butt of a pistol.

"You won't be needing that."

"That's smart."

"Hey, what's with the accent?" Knuckles asked. "This might not be the best neighborhood for you. Mexican or something?"

"Definitely not," the man said and pulled back his hood. His black, shoulder-length hair came into view. His irises were dark brown, but the dilated pupils made them look black.

"A beaner for sure," Knuckles said, getting to his feet. "There's nothing for you in that store."

"I think there is, but I have something to ask you two first."

"We aren't here to fuck around," Shade said.

"Neither am I. Do you know where I got this backpack?" the man asked. He swung it off his shoulder and tossed it to the ground a foot from Shade's shoes. Knuckles drew his gun.

"No idea. Goodwill?"

"Try again. The number on the shoulder strap might help."

Shade nudged the bag with his foot and saw the number eleven. He thought about it and then looked at Knuckles.

"Looks like Ty can't keep his damn mouth shut. We'll head over to his house after we're done here."

"No. You won't," the man said. "Ty is done working for you."

"Obviously you are way out of your league here, Spic."

"That's unnecessary."

"Hey, Shade. He's got pointy ears. He's one of those Dracs. Probably think they can take over our territory."

"Ain't no way that's going to happen."

"I'm not part of the group you mentioned. I would never stoop to such things. However, I do hope that this territory will be mine quite soon."

Knuckles raised his gun and squeezed the trigger. He got three shots off before he felt a pair of hot hands grip his head from behind and give it a violent twist. He was dead before he hit the ground.

Shade didn't even have time to react. The man broke both of his knees and watched him crumple to the ground.

"Fuck!" Shade yelled, grabbing at his ruined knees.

"Where's Frank?" he asked in a calm tone but noticed the old man inside the store coming around the counter. He had a gun in his hand.

"My knees!"

"Where's Frank? I won't ask again."

"What the hell is going on out here?" Chuck asked, as he reached the front door of the store.

"I'm trying to find Frank."

"You don't want that. Now, you get out of here. No one else needs to get hurt."

"Actually, yes. They do," the man said and punched Shade in the side of the head. His skull hit the concrete and sounded like a watermelon splitting open.

"Holy shit!" Chuck yelled, bringing his gun up. His hands were shaking, so he couldn't aim the weapon.

"Stay calm, answer my question, and you'll be fine. Where is Frank?"

"His guy pays me a hundred to use the store room."

"For what?"

"I don't know. They talk about stuff in there."

"Good. When was the last time you saw him?"

"He's in there right now. The boys that work for him show up around eight."

"Lower your gun before you hurt someone."

"No way I'm letting you do that to me or anyone else," Chuck said, motioning toward Shade. "I'm not afraid to shoot."

"Yes, you are, but let's just say it doesn't matter if you shoot or not."

Chuck pulled his trigger, and the bullet pierced the door of an old sedan across the street. The man was gone for a moment, but then reappeared in front of Chuck. He shoved him and the old man flew backwards into the store, crashing through a shelf full of Lay's potato chips. The door to the back room flew open. Stretch came out to see what had happened.

"Chuck?" he asked before noticing the man at the front door. "What are you doing?"

Chuck groaned and rolled off the pile of chips. He pointed toward the door, but he was having trouble catching his breath. Stretch looked up and saw the man.

"Frank! Get out the back!"

Suddenly, the man was in front of him.

"I don't think so," the man said. He was six inches shorter than Stretch. That gave him a good angle to punch through his sternum and crush his heart.

In the next instant, Barney lost his head. Frank dove to the ground, not knowing what was happening. The man moved over him.

"What are you?" Frank asked, cowering against the back exit.

"You'd never believe me. Besides, you aren't worth talking to anyway. You use teenagers to deal your drugs. If they get caught, they are still juveniles. They get lesser sentences, and you get another boy to take their place."

"I don't know what you're talking about!"

The man raised his left leg and stomped down on Frank's right ankle. There was a grinding sound as the bones crumbled to pieces.

"God!"

"No. That won't help. Tell me you're sorry."

"For what?"

The man stomped down on the other ankle, decimating those bones, too. Frank screamed in agony. The man waited.

"Are you sorry?"

"Yes. Yes! Whatever you want me to say! Just don't hurt me anymore."

"You think I should let you go?"

"Please, yes, I'll stop selling drugs, if that's what you want! I promise."

"Hmm," the man said. "Your word holds no value to me, but I want to make sure you don't keep up your business. Only one way to make sure of that."

"No!"

The man pivoted slightly and delivered a vicious side kick. Frank's head collapsed against the thick, steel emergency exit door. The man pulled back his foot and shook off some tissue that stuck to the sole. He walked out of the store room and saw Chuck trying to dial 911.

"You go ahead and call the police," the man said. "I'll let you live. The catch is that if I hear even a hint of you allowing another drug dealer to use your store for their work, I'll be back. I'll kill you. I'll kill your family. I'll burn this building to the ground. Got it?"

"Yes," Chuck whispered.

"When they show up, you tell those boys to get rid of the drugs or I'll find them. You tell them they can keep whatever money they have. Find a new job. Anything besides dealing."

"Okay."

"Good," the man said, and then he was gone.

He raced along the streets, eventually stopping near the Mississippi River at the entrance to the McKinley Bridge. He took a deep breath and glanced down at his boot, which still had a chunk of Frank's skull caught in the laces.

"Nice work," said a woman's voice from his right.

He looked up and took a defensive stance.

"I am Antonia. I'm leading the committee overseeing the competition to decide the next Overlord for this territory."

"Were you watching me?"

"Doing research and talking to the boy, Ty, first was a nice touch. His mom called the police as soon as you left, and we had people monitoring those lines."

"And you found me here?"

"I followed you here from the store," she said. "You're quick."

"I didn't hear you."

"That doesn't mean it didn't happen," Antonia said. "The Council owns the penthouse apartment at One Cardinal Way. You are expected to report there at ten in the morning. Get some rest or whatever tonight, but don't do any more work. No points will be awarded, and you will only make the competition harder if you draw more attention. Your claim is duly noted."

"Am I the first?"

"No, there is one other. There is still time for more to arrive and make a claim."

"Who was first?"

"Don't worry about that now. Be at the penthouse tomorrow morning and you will learn what you need to know."

"Fine."

"Thank you," she said. "Your name?"

"Etzli."

"Very good. It means blood. Right?"

"It does."

Antonia nodded and disappeared. He heard a car alarm to the south and assumed she must have set it off on her way by. He strolled south along the river, hoping to get a room at Horseshoe St. Louis Casino. He liked gambling.

13

"So, I finally got to sleep, and my phone started ringing," Fergus said. "I stayed up trying to finish season two of Breaking Bad."

"Wait," the man sitting next to him said, "you're just now watching Breaking Bad?"

"I'm trying to tell a story, Sam!"

"Sam? Jesus, man."

"Oh, right… sorry, Mungo."

"No real names, dumbass."

"I said I was sorry! Besides, we're in a safe spot."

"Doesn't matter."

"Get over it."

"You'll be the death of us."

"Can you two shut up?" Lucy asked. "It's one in the morning and I can't deal with your childish antics right now."

"Sorry, Mom," Fergus said.

"I'd stab you if the Count would allow it," she said.

"I know."

"But you really haven't seen Breaking Bad?" Mungo asked.

"Fuck my life," Lucy said.

"We can talk shows later, dude. So, my phone starts ringing, and I know it's important because the ringtone is Beethoven's Fifth."

"My god," Lucy said and flipped the hood of her jacket up.

"What? It's a good one. Besides, I know that it's Helsing when I hear it."

Lucy stood, picked up her coffee, and walked to the far corner of the room. She didn't even glance back. Instead, she picked up an old magazine and started flipping through it. Mungo was built like a lineman for a college football team. The chairs were too small for him, so he shifted in an attempt to get comfortable.

"What's her problem?" Fergus asked.

"You," Mungo said.

"I think she was equally pissed at you."

"Hey, guys," Ozul said, as he took a seat at the table in the antechamber across from Fergus. His curly blonde hair was normally in a perfectly groomed state, but he was wearing a solid black ball cap.

"Have you seen Breaking Bad?" Mungo asked him.

"Sure. Finished it a long time ago. That last episode was sweet. When he…"

"Shut up, Ozul!"

"What?"

"He is still on season two."

"Well, bad news for you, we are past the 'no spoiler' window on that."

"Can you two focus?" Fergus asked.

"On?"

"I was trying to tell a story about my night and Mungo totally sidetracked me with this Breaking Bad stuff."

"So, tell your story," Ozul said. He popped the top on a can of beer.

"I don't remember now. I knew I needed to hurry up and get here because Helsing was calling. Anyway, you all ruined it."

"Sounds like a shit story to me," Mungo said.

"You wouldn't know a good story if it slapped you in the face."

Five more people entered the room. Two sat at the other end of the table and three stood in a small circle near the door. That completed the group of eighteen. The door opened again, and Helsing stepped in.

"Good morning, everyone," he said. "The Count appreciates your promptness. Please make your way to his chamber to discuss today's events."

"Leave your beer in here," Fergus said to Ozul.

"Ozul can bring his drink," Helsing said.

"But I can't?"

"Absolutely not. You spill too often. The Count despises messes."

"It was only twice!"

"That's his decision."

"Fine."

"Lucy," Helsing said, "do you have the finances?"

"Do I ever NOT have the finances?"

"I'll let that go since you look like you haven't slept."

"I look like… never mind."

"Good, now, let's go in," he said and started along the dark hallway with red light bulbs. The heavy steel door marking the entrance to the Count's chamber slid open with a rumble, but no squeaks. "Find your seats, please."

No sooner had the last person taken their seat than the Count strode in from his own entrance. The blacklights along the wall reflected off the trim on his cape. Helsing pulled out the chair at the head of the table and their leader sat.

"Greetings," he said.

"Good morning, Count," they said together.

"Have any of you heard about the news today?"

"I heard about a vampire-themed murder in north city," one of the women said.

"Also, an attack on an auto body shop near midtown," Fergus said.

"Good," the Count said. "I appreciate that you all are listening to what is going on."

"But, sir," Claudia, the woman who had commented before, said, "My info says that the one old man that survived said it was a vampire. It wasn't us, was it?"

"No, Claudia, it was not. Does anyone have ideas about this?"

"Could it have been someone from one of our crews going rogue?" Mungo asked.

"I would hope not," the Count said. "Each of you has better control of your people than that, right? That was rhetorical. Of course, you do, or I'd have you removed in a less than graceful way."

"Yes, sir," Mungo said.

"Anything else? Romeo?"

"Someone is trying to take advantage of our hard work and momentum. Maybe they thought they could swoop in and make some easy money on our backs?" asked the man at the far end of the table. He was wearing all black leather with black eyeliner and his jet-black hair was gelled firmly to his head. He looked the part, but his seat showed that he was the least productive of the group.

"Perhaps," the Count said. "Any thoughts on this idea?"

"Nothing was stolen from the old man's shop."

"Nothing?" Romeo asked.

"The auto shop was the same. Nothing stolen, but there is quite a bit of blood to clean up," Fergus said.

"So, I guess that rules out that idea," the Count said.

"Yes, sir," Romeo said.

"There is one more scenario that might fit," the Count said, looking from face to face. "What if more of the vampires, like the one I killed, have come to town?"

"Are there more of them?" Fergus asked.

"Almost certainly. It is only logical that there would be more."

"Right."

"So, what do we do if this is correct?" the Count said.

"We monitor all police activity even more closely than normal. We respond to anything that sounds suspicious. I expect regular reporting to Helsing with any news. We have to be careful in our hunt," Lucy said in an even tone. "Rocky and his guys proved that we are vulnerable if we aren't careful."

"Excellent point, Lucy. I'm putting you in charge of keeping track of communications. Helsing has too much on his plate to handle more of that. You will filter what everyone else feeds you and send the important things up to him."

"As you wish, sir."

"Good. Does that work for you, Helsing?"

"Of course."

"Sir, can I ask a question?" Ozul asked.

"Certainly."

"Should we follow up on both of today's robberies to make sure nothing was stolen? The old man at the store might not have checked close enough if he was shook up. I would hate to see us overreact."

"It would be a mistake to underreact, too," Claudia said. "My contact was confident that nothing was taken."

"But you'll follow up anyway," the Count said.

"Yes, sir," Claudia said.

"Good. Now, I need to know if there are any other questions or concerns."

There was silence as they watched him. He studied each face in turn, finishing with Helsing in the chair to his right. No one commented.

"This is your chance. You all know I'm open to thoughts and ideas. That is the only way to have a successful organization. For our regular meeting next week, I want at least one way to increase money flow from each of you. The more detailed the better. If you have something good, we will implement it, and it could affect the order of chairs."

The Count stood and they all did, too. Helsing moved to pull out his chair.

"Get some rest. My apologies for calling this meeting so late, but this was important."

"Anything you wish, sir," Helsing said.

The Count nodded and looked around the room once more. Then, he spun and walked out of the room. His cape flowed behind him.

"That concludes tonight's meeting," Helsing said. "Please make your way out of the building. The antechamber is closed for the night."

"Got it," Lucy said and started for the door.

The others fell in behind her. Fergus and Mungo were the last ones out. They went up the stairs and out the former emergency exit into the alley. Fergus lit a cigarette.

"What do you think about those attacks?" Mungo asked.

"I don't know," Fergus said. "I'm going to be watching my ass. I can tell you that. Did you see what happened to Rocky and Merle?"

"I didn't want to. Was it bad?"

"Man, you have no idea. It looked like something out of a Saw movie."

"Damn."

"I don't want to end up like that," Fergus said. "I mean, I trust the plan and all that, but I didn't really understand what these vampires could do."

"Hell, I didn't know they were real. I thought it was some sort of show. Kinda like the Count."

"Man, don't let him or Helsing hear you say that."

"I know."

Fergus took a deep drag on his cigarette and blew out a cloud. He stared up into the light-polluted sky.

"What are you doing now?" Mungo asked.

"I don't know. Going home?"

"I'm not tired. Let's hit a bar."

"Don't they all close in an hour?"

"Not if you know the right ones," Mungo said. "I'm going even if you don't."

"Fine. I'll go for a bit. I'll sleep in tomorrow. I've got nowhere to be."

"Good," the big man said, slapping Fergus on the shoulder. "Meet me at Ashley's Place. It's in Soulard."

"I've been there."

Thunder echoed down the alley and large raindrops hit the pavement. Mungo pulled his coat shut and turned up the collar.

"Let's go, then," Mungo said. "I don't want to melt."

"What are you? Five?"

"So, Walter White…"

"Shut up. Let's go."

14

Eztli spent the night playing roulette and poker. A major perk of this territory for him was the options for enjoying the nightlife. Compared to most of the other gamblers, his funds were nearly unlimited. That earned him some quick friends, including two members of the St. Louis City board of aldermen. He hoped to earn some extra points in the competition by having connections to decision-makers among the humans.

"Not bad," he said as he walked along Washington Street shortly after dawn. He was admiring the older buildings and anticipating taking control of the city. "I think this will work."

"You can come visit," said a man behind him. Eztli turned to look. A tall, thin, pale man looked back. "I'm Jaroslaw."

"I am Eztli. I assume you are here to make a claim?"

"Indeed. I believe there is more than enough for the two of us. Our predecessor held more territory than most Overlords hold presently."

"That's true," Eztli said.

"So, how do you feel about redistributing the territory?"

"Logically, we could divide things into two or three pieces. However, I understand the intrigue of challenging for a huge territory. The profits for the current alignment would be massive."

"If we split geographically, there would be an easy solution."

"But Chicago is a far superior area and can't possibly be included in an even split as far as land."

"So, you are opposed to an east to west split?"

"Whoever gets the east part will come out way ahead."

"That is what those in charge would have you believe."

"Okay. Then, I'll take the eastern half," Eztli said.

"No, I don't think that would be fair."

"And there we have it."

"So, we can't agree on an even geographical split?"

"Obviously not if you want the better half."

"I guess the competition continues," Jaroslaw said and started toward their destination.

"Apparently so. Let's go on to the penthouse and see what the committee has for us."

"Have you been to the baseball stadium?"

"I haven't, but the game does nothing for me. How about you?"

"Nah, it's boring. Soccer, as they call it, or la crosse is much better."

"Agreed," Etzli said.

"Are you a tea or coffee person?"

"Coffee for sure. Tea is so European," Eztli said and took out his phone. He tapped the Chrome icon and then typed in his search. "There is a Starbucks near here."

"I'm not impressed with their offerings."

"There aren't any other options nearby. Unless you want to go to one of the hotel restaurants."

"Starbucks will be fine for today," Jaroslaw said. "Besides, it will give us a chance to observe the people of the city in a more relaxed setting."

"Relaxed? I don't think you've been to an American Starbucks, but let's go."

They walked along the sidewalk with an increasing number of people going to work. They took a turn at the end of the second block and then another when they reached Chestnut Street.

The line of people waiting for a drink twisted along the display of coffee, before ducking behind a pillar. The end of the line was a woman in a blue dress. She saw them approach. Eztli's thick curly hair hid the tips of his ears, but Jaroslaw's long brown hair fell around his ears. She locked her gaze on them and then looked back at him. She shook her head and turned her back.

"This city is going to be a public relations nightmare," Eztli said.

"Why do you care what they think? They're just food."

"That's oversimplifying it. They also bring in plenty of money for us to continue improving our business. Besides, if the area is more desirable to them, then the better humans will move in. That leads to better meat."

"Yes, I suppose you are right," Jaroslaw said and opened the glass door.

They waited in line for nearly half an hour.

"Ezra Lee?" called one of the baristas. "Caramel Macchiato for Ezra Lee?"

"Eztli."

"Oh. Have a great day!"

Jaroslaw was already at a high top table at the back of the store. He had a Venti Pike Place with a shot of espresso.

"That's a fancy drink."

"That Pike Place tastes like dirt."

"You're not wrong, but most of the coffee here does."

"Fair enough," Eztli said. "So, what is your plan for the territory if you win?"

"When I win, I will clean up this city and get it back in order. Then, I will make sure each of my deputies understands that I will be running a tighter ship, so to speak."

"Headquarters?"

"I think Chicago has been the main city for many years. I don't see a reason to change that."

"I want to take a tour of the entire territory before deciding on where I would live. Living the nomad life for the last few hundred years has grown boring. I hope to build an estate of some sort. Definitely in the tradition of my homeland."

"Where is that?"

"It predates the current nations, but the city of La Paz is a short journey from where I was born. My family lived in the mountains north of where the city is."

"Near Lake Titicaca, then?" Jaroslaw asked, the corner of his mouth turning up.

"My, my," Eztli said. "This newer generation has had so much fun with our lake's name."

"I don't blame them. It's amusing."

"And where are you from?"

"Originally, I lived in a castle outside of Minsk. The humans call it Mir castle and most of them believe it was built for one of their own lords. I still visit from time to time, but it has been over a hundred years since I was there last. I heard they added a restaurant to it."

"These humans and their schemes," Eztli said and sipped his drink.

He laughed. The woman in the blue dress looked over at him.

"Do you think the competition will be between us?"

"It does look that way."

"We should probably make our way to the penthouse soon."

"Agreed. I am curious to meet this committee that will be deciding our fate."

They both stood and started for the door. Eztli caught the woman's gaze and held it until he was even with her. He gave a wink, and she flushed, looking away from him. Their destination was only two blocks away. They had plenty of time.

"Ballpark Village," Eztli said, as they walked across the parking lot for the tower. "That looks like an interesting place."

"Maybe for you."

"Something to do at least. What are you going to do today?"

"I plan on starting my research into the city. There seems to be many distinct neighborhoods in the older part of the city. I want to know more about where this competition will be held."

"Not a bad plan, and I wish you the best. I might check things out later this evening. I prefer to operate after dark."

"How cliché of you," Jaroslaw said and opened the door. "After you."

A man in a red suit sat at a raised desk near the elevator. He wore a matching hat and was studying a small bank of monitors. He looked up as they approached.

"Good morning, gentlemen," he said. "How can I help you today?"

Jaroslaw sniffed the air once and looked to Eztli.

"A commoner. How nice."

"I'm sorry, sir?"

"We are here on business in the penthouse," Jaroslaw said and brushed his hair behind his ears with his fingertips.

"Oh, yes, my apologies," the man said. He took two plastic cards from his desk and held them out. "These will get you to the penthouse. The last elevator will take you up."

"Thank you, my good man," Jaroslaw said.

They each took a card and walked to the nearest elevator. Eztli pushed the button, and they waited. They were sure the man at the desk was watching them. No doubt that seeing nomads was rare for him.

Neither of them came up with anything to say as they rode up. The situation seemed more formal all of a sudden. They both tried to imagine what was waiting for them. The doors opened.

"Greetings," Antonia said. She was standing ten feet in front of them. She wore a plain black dress that fell to her ankles. A solid black cloak with gold lining hung gently from her shoulders. The hood was down.

"Good morning," they said.

"Please, join me in the conference area."

She did not wait for a response, instead turning and walking briskly to their left. A broad mahogany table stood near a large window. They were able to look down into Busch Stadium and across the southern part of the city.

"An impressive view," Eztli said.

"This?" Antonia said, looking out the window as if she hadn't done that yet. "I suppose so. Anyway, please take a seat in one of the white chairs."

The five white chairs were on the long side of the table facing the window. Five matching chairs with red upholstery were on the opposite side. A single red chair held spots at the ends of the table.

Antonia went to the center chair on the red side and lifted her arms. A male and female figure emerged from a door to her left and another pair from her right. They took up their places behind the chairs on her side. The men wore solid black suits and women had on dresses to match Antonia. Their cloaks had a red lining, instead of gold.

"Please, sit," Antonia said. Jaroslaw moved first, taking the center chair. He wanted to face her. Eztli took the seat immediately to his left, not wanting the chair to the right. He thought it might make him look like an assistant rather than a competitor. The four cloaked figures sat. "Lights."

Blinds rolled down over the tall windows and the overhead lights dimmed. A projector came to life, shining the Queen's seal on the wall to their left. Antonia took a sip of water.

"Today is the day of information. We will go over the rules of the competition, present the territory to be claimed, and answer any questions you might have. Please refrain from asking anything until the end. We have been doing this for many years and the information will be covered thoroughly."

Eztli and Jaroslaw nodded their understanding.

"First, I want to introduce you to the committee. To my far right is Ahmed. His origin is the Nile Valley," Antonia said. Ahmed stood, offered a quick bow, and then sat. The others would follow suit. "Next is Jiemba. Her origin in the island now known as Australia. Xue is here to my left. She is from western China. Finally, Einar. He is Scandinavian. As you know, my name is Antonia. I have led these committees for nearly three centuries, working closely with Queen Stephanie. I am originally from what you know as Sicily."

She held up her hand and clicked the remote she held. The picture transitioned to a map showing the central third of the United States and part of Canada.

"The area in pink is the territory you are competing for. It is one of the largest territories still intact. The Queen has debated splitting it but did not see the need at this point. The territory includes the southern portion of Manitoba, southwestern Ontario. In the United States, you will have most of the Dakotas, Nebraska, Kansas. The territory also includes the states of Illinois, Wisconsin, Minnesota, Missouri, and Iowa. Yes, it is a lot to manage but is doable with the right team. The victor will have to make smart decisions. Your life could depend on it.

"Next is scoring. There is no scoring. We will all keep track of how your actions make us feel about your competency to run the territory. Being an Overlord requires the ability to do what needs to be done and figuring out how to do it the best way possible. There are three basic rules that cannot be violated, or your claim is forfeit. First, you cannot leave the territory once the competition has begun. Second, you may not harm any of the other competitors. Finally, you may not enlist help from those outside the competition to improve your position.

"There is still most of one full day left for other nomads to make their claim and enter the competition. They must complete an act that shows their interest, as you both did. Then, they must arrive here before ten tomorrow morning. We are not anticipating any other competitors at this time.

"Finally, the deputies of the previous Overlord, Kenny McClelland, have maintained order in all other parts of the territory. Because this city is facing uncertainty, we have decided to hold the competition here. Now, do you have any questions?"

"Can we work together?" Eztli asked.

"If you wish."

"Is there an ultimate task which will help our claim more than others?" Jaroslaw asked.

"As I stated, there is no scoring. Do what you think would be best if you were in charge of the territory."

Neither of them came up with any other questions.

"Very well. You should arrive here no later than nine tomorrow. The competition will officially begin at ten."

"Do any other competitors have to be here at nine?" Eztli asked.

"They must simply be here by ten. You should arrive an hour early so that we can be prompt with starting things off. You will both be able to start the competition immediately at ten. If they arrive close to the start time, they will have to sit through the information while you have already started."

"Sounds fair."

"Yes, it does," Antonia said. "Now, if neither of you has any more questions, you are dismissed until tomorrow morning. Remember that we will be watching you only to make sure you do not start early. You will not see us, but we will be there."

The projector turned off and the blinds went up. Jaroslaw and Eztli stood, bowed as the others had, and went to the elevator. None of the committee moved until the doors closed.

The two competitors stood quietly as they went down. When they went outside, Jaroslaw offered his hand to Eztli.

"Here is where we go our own ways, I believe," he said.

"I will see you tomorrow."

15

Jaroslaw walked through the front doors of One Cardinal Way at twenty minutes until nine the following morning. He hated being late. The same commoner was sitting at the desk.

"Welcome back, sir," he said.

"Thank you. Will my card work today?"

"Yes. The card will work until the committee instructs us to deactivate it."

"Will that be after the competition?"

"I am here to manage access to the building. The committee doesn't tell me or my coworkers anything more than that."

"Ah, I see. I'm going to go upstairs, then."

"Very good, sir."

Jaroslaw walked over to the last set of doors and pushed the button. He was surprised when they opened immediately. It was vacant, so he stepped in. Moments later, the doors reopened at the penthouse.

No one was there to greet him. Einar, one of the committee members, was standing near the windows. His platinum blonde hair glowed in the half-light. Jaroslaw started across the main room, but noticed Eztli seated in a red, oversized, plush chair to his right. There were four of those chairs around a white, marble table, so he joined him.

"Good morning," he said, drawing Eztli's attention.

"Ah, yes, welcome. How was your evening?"

"Quite tame, actually. The city is less than three hundred years old, so I got through its history in half a night. The rest of the territory will take a bit longer. The natives who lived here before the white settlers will require more research."

"Interesting. What about the rest of the territory?"

"It appears to be a recurring theme."

"That makes sense, I suppose," Eztli said. "South America is much the same, but the so-called settlers were not quite as invasive. You should get some coffee from the bar over there. It is delicious. Much better than that swill we had yesterday."

"Thank you. I'll get a cup now," he said and went to get a mug for himself. He looked over the cream and sugar options but ultimately took it black. He returned and chose the seat across from Eztli. "Have you seen any other competitors?"

"Not yet. I've only seen the Norseman and the woman in the purple dress so far."

"What woman?" Jaroslaw said, turning in his chair to scan the room. He saw her in a shadowed corner looking out at the city. She was deep in thought, but the look on her face made her seem unapproachable. "I completely missed her when I came in. Did she talk to you?"

"No. I have no idea what her role is in this."

"Should we invite her over?"

"You can, but I think I'll wait for the committee."

"Okay," Jaroslaw said. He studied the woman a moment longer and then took out his phone to continue his research.

The hands on the large wall clock slipped past nine and dropped toward the bottom of the hour. Eztli was lost in thought and Jaroslaw continued reading about the territory. They both looked up when they heard the elevator ding.

"Welcome back," Einar said, walking toward the elevator. Antonia stepped out and met him halfway across the room. "Is she here?"

"She will be up in a matter of minutes. Let the others know."

Antonia was in her plain black dress but did not have her cloak on. Jiemba emerged from one of the side rooms. She was wearing her cloak and had Antonia's gold-lined cloak draped over her right arm. The head of the committee turned to allow Jiemba to put the cloak on her. She adjusted it to make sure it hung perfectly and then tied the strap that held the shoulders together across the base of her neck.

The elevator door gave another ding. The remainder of the committee came into the room with their cloaks already on. Each took the same spot behind the table that they had occupied the day before. A black woman wearing a plain white t-shirt and blue jeans stepped out of the elevator. Her hair hung down her back in thick braids. She held a large, clear plastic bag in each hand.

Jaroslaw and Eztli stood, knowing they had more competition after all. Neither could make out what was in the bags. They moved in her direction but paused when Antonia spoke.

"Greetings," she said. "Welcome to the penthouse. You have completed your act to make your claim. Please give us your name."

"My name is Kiona. I am originally from a small village on the western bank of Lake Victoria."

"Very good. Your claim is recorded, and you are hereby admitted to the competition. What do you have with you?"

"It is tradition where I am from to bring a gift to special occasions," Kiona said. "I have brought you a pair of vests from these Dracs that are plaguing this city."

"Vests?" Eztli asked. He meant for it to be under his breath, but his voice carried across the room. Everyone turned to look at him.

"To be clear," Kiona said, "The vests contain the torsos of two of the Dracs. I removed their arms, legs, and heads to make for a better trophy. I used the plastic bags to make sure their blood did not stain the carpets."

Antonia offered a polite smile and said, "An excellent gift. Thank you. On behalf of the committee, I would like you to present them to our guest, Celia. She is the mother of the previous Overlord for this territory."

Celia nodded and walked over to Kiona. She looked down at the bags and then took them. She stepped back four paces before speaking.

"I appreciate this gift," she said. "My Hans did not deserve the end he got, and this is a perfect first step for you in laying claim to his territory. In case any of the competitors are wondering, I will not be part of the committee choosing his successor. My request to the committee was to be allowed to participate in the opening of the competition. A request that Antonia most graciously granted."

"It is our pleasure to have you here today," Antonia said.

"If I might, I'd like to put these with my things in the next room. I'll be ready to view the start of the competition after that."

"We still have twenty-two minutes until the start."

Celia offered a quick bow of her head. She turned and went through one of the doors to the left of the elevator. Kiona looked toward Eztli and Jaroslaw. She decided to join them.

"Welcome, I'm Jaroslaw."

"And I'm Eztli."

"Blood?" Kiona asked. "I like it."

"Thank you."

"If I might suggest something," Jaroslaw said, "I was waiting until close to the time of the competition to see who all was competing and I think it will be the three of us. This territory is massive, and I believe we could divide it up between us to avoid the competition entirely. The allotted land would be more than enough for three or more territories in Europe."

"How would you split it?"

"There are clear benefits to some areas over others. I would propose that I take the Illinois and Wisconsin areas. The two of you could split the rest. I would suggest an agreed upon east to west line dividing it in half."

"That would give you Chicago," Eztli said.

"True, but it would be a much smaller territory."

"Easily the most profitable, though," Kiona said.

"There is great potential in all the areas of this territory."

"Perhaps I could take Chicago, and you could have one of the halves," Eztli said.

"I don't really want to do that," Jaroslaw said.

"Then, I believe we have a consensus," Kiona said. "We will continue with the competition, as planned."

"Agreed," Eztli said.

"Very well," Jaroslaw said and returned to his chair.

At precisely ten o'clock, Antonia began the competition.

"Please, competitors, join us at the table."

Jaroslaw was disgruntled over the rejection of his plan and walked ahead of the others. He took the center chair, like the day before. Kiona took the far right chair, leaving a seat between hers and Jaroslaw. Eztli stopped behind the chair he had used before and then moved down one, creating balance on their side of the table.

"Everyone sit, please," Antonia said. The other committee members and the competitors sat. "As of this moment, the competition is underway. The judging begins as soon as I conclude this meeting. Eztli and Jaroslaw, you will be free to begin your work when I release you. Kiona, due to your late arrival, I must ask you to stay and listen to the information we gave the others yesterday."

Kiona nodded to her.

"There is no set end to the timeframe of the competition. Only the committee can declare it to be over. Understood?"

"Yes," they said together.

"Without further ado, let's begin. Jaroslaw and Eztli, you are both dismissed. Remember, the committee will be watching, however, we will not participate in the event."

Eztli and Jaroslaw stood, looked at each other and went to the elevator. Jaroslaw pushed the button and the door opened. They rode down together. Kiona joined the competition about thirty minutes later.

16

"Tonight is an important night. We have exactly one hour until the raid begins. We must all move at the same time. This is a bold plan, but taking down a police precinct will show them that the Dracs are in charge. There will be casualties on both sides. Anyone inside the building is fair game, but focus on the officers," Claudia said from her spot at the end of the table in the antechamber. "I'm going to take two resources with me in the Mobile Control Center."

"Two people in the van?" Romeo asked.

"You know the Count expects us to use the correct terminology. It's more than just a van, and the regular Dracs are nothing more than resources to him. Right?"

"Right."

"Okay. So, I'll take the Mobile Control Center with two resources. Fergus, how many do you have lined up and where are they waiting?"

"I have seventeen ready to go at the Tilles Park Pavilion."

"Mungo?"

"Twenty-two at Sublette Park near the tennis courts."

"Romeo?"

"I have thirty-six in a holding pattern outside the YMCA."

"A holding pattern?" Fergus asked. "Are they airplanes?"

"Shut up, Fergus," Romeo said.

"Did you say the YMCA?" Claudia asked.

"Yes."

"But not the South City YMCA."

"Well, yeah. The instructions said to find a public place that wasn't too far away."

"They also said to stay away from the precinct and the YMCA is across the street in plain view. You are an idiot. Please don't tell me they are sitting out in the open."

Romeo didn't respond.

"Jesus."

"I feel bad for your resources, Romeo."

"Shut up, Fergus."

"Anyway," Claudia said, "Mungo, I want you to bring your group in on Harlequin and come across the back parking lot. You should target the delivery entrance on the north end. It will be the biggest challenge since we know it is a steel door instead of glass like the others."

"We will be in place when the other two teams hit the building. Someone will panic and come out that way."

"Good. Fergus, your group should park at the corner of Jasper and Connecticut. The house at that corner doesn't have a fence, so you can get behind the houses on Connecticut and cut through to the south end of the parking lot. You will take the primary back entrance. It's glass, but it will be locked."

"No problem."

"And Romeo. Front entrance. The doors will be unlocked, of course, but you'll draw the first attention."

"Where should we park?"

"Your group is literally across the road. How are you even in the Count's favor?"

"Don't question the Count," Romeo said.

"I can't imagine you'll make it through this," Claudia said. "So, it'll be a non-issue."

"I could take you down anytime."

"Try it."

"Can we focus here?" Fergus asked. "Clock's ticking and all that."

"Yes, it is," Claudia said. "Everyone get to your places and wait for my signal. I want everyone to hit the building at nine sharp."

"We'll be ready," Fergus said.

"Then, let's go," she said.

Mungo led the way. Fergus waited for Romeo to go out so that he didn't try anything with Claudia. She went to the small metal cabinet on the wall and took out a set of keys. Her vest was on a hook near the door. She slipped it on, glanced in the mirror, and took a deep breath.

"This is your big night. Time to move up."

She went up the stairs and out along the sidewalk that led to a garage that the Count owned on the next lot. She swung open a small silver door to access a keypad. Six digits later, the overhead door began to climb.

A black Chevy panel van was one of the six vehicles stored in the long narrow building. It was in the last spot because of the technology it held. The Count didn't want anyone to use it unless absolutely necessary.

Claudia started the engine, activated the auxiliary power bank for the computers, and checked to make sure it was all working. She pulled out onto the street, punched the remote to close the garage door, and headed west.

When she pulled into the lot at The Home Depot off Kingshighway south of Tower Grove Park, she didn't see any vehicles following her. She selected a spot near Sonic that would allow for a quick exit if she needed it. She dialed her phone.

"I'm here," she said.

"Be right out."

Claudia went to the back of the van and started her rundown of tasks. A knock came at the side door. She opened it to see two younger men in matching black sweatshirts and jeans.

"Feels weird not to have our vests on," the first one said.

"Well, Ronald, that's part of working undercover. We don't want to draw the attention that the vests promise. Now, get in here. Harold, I want you on the communication system. Ronald, you take the drone. Keep it high enough to avoid attention, but make sure I can clearly see the whole property at once."

"Got it," they said and got to work. Ronald opened the back door and set out the drone. Then, he hurried to his designated computer and sent it to the sky. Harold had things running in under a minute.

"How much time?" Harold asked.

"Eighteen minutes."

"When do we move them into position?"

"Soon."

"Is Claudia your real name?"

"What?"

"I've heard that those in the Count's inner group have code names. Just wondering if you were one of those people."

"I am."

"Why don't we get code names?"

"I need you to focus on the task in front of you. Don't get distracted. Someday you might earn a seat at the table."

"That'd be cool," Ronald said.

"Yes," she said.

She turned her attention to the monitor on the wall. The drone was moving over the city. They sat in silence until Claudia sat up straight in her seat and took her radio.

"Readiness check," she said. "Romeo?"

"Ready."

"Fergus?"

"Ready."

"Mungo?"

"Ready, m'lady."

"Kiss-ass," Fergus said.

"Nothing extra on the radio," Claudia said. "We have ten minutes until go time. Mungo and Fergus, I want you to move your people into position. Make sure everyone has their vests or coats on. The Count's emblem needs to show up on every camera tonight."

"We're all set," Fergus said.

"Same here," Mungo said.

"One minute," Romeo said. "Terry is looking for his vest."

"He's going with or without the vest."

"Understood."

"Romeo. Start moving your people toward the building. You'll draw attention, but I want you in place before the others come in."

"Got it," he said.

Claudia watched the screen as his group started moving across to the YMCA parking lot. She was glad to see they were jogging into place. She thought maybe Romeo did understand how critical speed was on this.

She looked at the time in the corner of the screen and said, "Five, four, three, two, one… GO!"

Both groups from the back of the building moved toward their designated spots and Romeo's group raced along the crosswalk. They flooded the front sidewalk and went to the building. There was one civilian outside the front door. He dropped his cigarette and ran north away from the building.

Terry was one of the first two people to the double glass doors. They flung the doors open, and the crowd pushed them back against the building. The closers protested for a second but then tore free from the metal doorframe.

As the group filled the lobby, the duty officer jumped to his feet.

"All officers to the front!" he yelled into a radio. "We're under attack!"

Four members of Romeo's group stepped forward with shotguns and let loose on the glass door that allowed access to the rest of the building, along with the plate separating the duty officer from them.

The glass shattered, but the metal mesh inside mostly held its shape. Three more officers appeared at the duty desk. Two more Dracs grabbed a bench from the waiting area and started beating them into the glass.

"What's the order?" one of the officers asked.

"If they get through, we shoot! The alert is out, and we'll have them surrounded shortly."

It took only four hits with the benches to knock one end of the mangled glass from its frame. The bench hung up in the mesh and the Dracs holding it tried pulling it back to allow access to the opening. Instead, an officer stepped into view and shot. The Drac on the left went down immediately with a shot to the head. The other twisted away when a bullet struck her in the shoulder.

"Push it through!" Romeo yelled.

The group of Dracs pushed forward. They drove the bench through the opening and the rest of the window went with it. The gaping hole was an invitation to battle. Seven officers were in the room to meet them. Shots rang out from both groups.

Fergus's group reached the back door on the south end as the shooting started. He went to the door first and aimed his ten gauge shotgun. He let loose five quick rounds focused at the hinges of the door. When he ducked away, two others stepped up with small grappling hooks on ropes. They put them through the shattered glass, moved back, and pulled in unison.

The door moved an inch or two. Two more pulls and the top of the door came free. Others rushed forward to grab it and take it from its frame. Three people in civilian clothes peeked out from offices along the hallway ahead of them. Two of them died when the Dracs opened fire. The other managed to get back inside.

The steel utility door flew open at the north end of the building. An older Hispanic man with thick, gray hair rushed out. He was wearing blue coveralls with the name Carlos on them. He held a broom in his right hand.

Mungo was at the head of his group. He grabbed the man by the coveralls and pulled him close. He stared into his eyes and saw absolute fear. Mungo grinned and tossed the man to the side. One of the other Dracs held the door. They were in.

Jaroslaw was sitting on a support bar about halfway up the communications tower at the back of the property. He watched the attack and considered how he would move in.

"Hey, there," Eztli said, appearing on the bar below him. Jaroslaw didn't flinch.

"Hello."

"Should we do this together? I have not heard anything from Kiona. Maybe she isn't here."

"She will be. These Dracs are noisy," Jaroslaw said, turning to look at him. "What are you wearing?"

"This?" Eztli asked, looking at his outfit. He had selected a mask with a cape and a gray body suit. "I saw a movie today and thought this would be appropriate."

"You're an idiot."

"No. I'm Batman."

"Let's go," Jaroslaw said and jumped down from his perch.

They raced inside and engaged the Dracs. Jaroslaw grabbed one unsuspecting victim who was looking away from him. He turned him around, looked him in the eye, and snapped his neck. Eztli was more dramatic, moving into the back of Mungo's group. He drove his fists through the backs of two Dracs and ripped out a handful of bloody innards.

The shots rang out between the cops and the Dracs. The officers were more prepared. They took out their attackers at a two-to-one ratio, but that was not fast enough.

One officer at the center of the building was taking aim over a desk when his target disappeared.

"What the hell?" he asked, scanning the area.

Suddenly, the woman he had been targeting landed on his desk. Her eyes were bulging, and it looked like her neck had been ripped open. A figure appeared near where he had been aiming.

"Batman?" he asked in disbelief.

"We've got sirens coming from all four quadrants," Harold said. "Should we call off the attack?"

"No."

"But they'll be wiped out when reinforcements arrive!"

"Acceptable," Claudia said.

Ronald stared at her, finally understanding how things worked.

"They're here!" Fergus yelled into his radio.

"Repeat that," Harold said.

"They're here! The vampires!"

"How many?"

"Not sure, but…"

"Fergus?" Harold asked and waited for a response. "Fergus?"

"Assume he's down," Claudia said. "Bring back the drone."

"Yes, ma'am," Ronald said.

There were two quick knocks on the van door.

"Who's that?" Harold asked.

"Someone being nosy. Stay focused," Claudia said.

Two more heavier knocks came next, and someone tried the handle.

"God damn it," Claudia said under her breath. Then, she yelled, "Go away!"

There was a boom and pop. The door screeched as it came off its track. Claudia grabbed a gun from the shelf next to her and turned just in time to see a black woman in a black hoodie. Her mouth opened in a wicked smile and Claudia froze. She couldn't look away from the fangs.

Kiona leaped into the van and grabbed Claudia by the shoulders. She bit into her neck, tearing her jugular out with a vicious twist. Her body slumped to the floor of the van, but Harold and Ronald met matching fates before Claudia came to rest.

"That should send the message," Kiona said. She looked over her victims before wiping her mouth with the back of her sleeve. She heard a crack outside and stepped out to look. The drone had smacked into the side of the van and landed on the asphalt. She looked down on it and her face appeared on the screen inside the van. The Count was watching a transmission of that feed.

17

Antonia sat at her desk in the penthouse. She looked out over the city, thinking about what she had in front of her. This was one small corner of the open territory, yet things were messier than she had seen in the biggest cities in some time.

The sun was rising behind her, allowing the tower to cast a shadow across the blocks in front of her. The rest of the committee would be arriving shortly to discuss the previous night's events, but she already had strong feelings about where things stood. The elevator dinged.

"Good morning," Jiemba said. Einar was to her left.

"It is a satisfactory morning," Antonia said, without looking at them.

"Would you like us in our cloaks for the meeting?"

"For our discussion it is unnecessary, but they are required for the meeting with the competitors."

"Would you like some coffee, Jiemba?" Einar asked.

"Sure. A splash of cream, but no sugar. Thank you."

Einar nodded and went to the coffee station. He took a raspberry scone after pouring both cups. Jiemba was waiting at the end of the long table they used for business. She had selected the chair furthest from Antonia.

Ahmed emerged from the hallway leading to the bedrooms. He had a book in his hand, walking with a steady swaying motion. Oblivious to his surroundings, he walked directly to one of the plush armchairs in the corner of the main room and sat without looking up from his book.

"Has anyone spoken to Xue this morning?" Antonia asked. Her voice was low and even, but it filled the space.

"I believe she was going to do some climbing," Ahmed said.

"Very well," Antonia said. "We will start as soon as she returns. Please begin gathering your thoughts on the competition."

"What are you reading, Ahmed?" Einar asked.

"I found it at a bookstore down the street. It's called 'What Others Won't Do' and it's a western. A quaint little story about what the Americans call the old west. I find the concept behind the story to be quite applicable to our current task."

"Mind if I read it when you're done?"

"That's fine with me."

Einar and Jiemba resumed a quiet discussion at the table. Ahmed went on reading. Antonia didn't move from her spot for five minutes.

"Please join me at the table," she said, rising from her chair.

"Are we waiting for Xue?" Jiemba asked.

Antonia did not respond. Instead, she walked to her seat at the center of the table, pulled her notepad close, and uncapped her pen. Seconds later, Xue's left hand appeared on the railing at the bottom of the balcony. She pulled herself up and swung her leg into the gap between the bars. From there she pushed herself to the top of the railing and slipped over. She took some deep breaths, looking out at the city, and then walked inside.

"We will start in three minutes," Antonia said.

"Thank you," Xue said.

She went to the kitchen and got a bottle of water. Ahmed laid his book on the side table and went to join the others. Jiemba and Einar assumed their assigned seats. Xue was the last to take their seat, but Antonia waited to start the discussion precisely three minutes after her announcement.

"Let's begin," she said. "Last night, we had the first major activity of the competition. All three contenders were involved. Interestingly enough, the Dracs did us the favor of planning their own attack that made for a good first event. I would like to hear each of your thoughts. Then, I will consolidate them and present them to the competitors. If you do not believe there is a clear leader amongst them, that's fine. Ahmed, please begin."

"The sheer force exhibited by two of the competitors, Eztli and Jaroslaw, was impressive. From what I could see, neither of them received even a scratch. They eliminated almost all of the Dracs at the police station in a matter of minutes. Jiemba?"

"The force doesn't impress me. That's easy enough when we are that much better than any human. I appreciated the surprise factor. The Dracs spent days planning this event, yet they seemed caught off guard by the competitors' attack. Xue?"

"Precision and patience are the most important things to me. I can appreciate that the Dracs lost a large number of people during the attack, but the fact remains that the Count is recruiting new people at a rapid pace. They did take out some of the people who were part of the Count's inner circle, but that was purely by chance since they wiped out everyone. The number of bystanders lost was also unacceptable. Einar?"

"I will build off Xue's thoughts, but I had a different take on the events. We are choosing someone to take over this territory. They will choose their own team to handle uprisings and such. The one competitor that has not been mentioned was the one who watched and waited. She tracked those in control of the entire event and eliminated them. Those people can be replaced, but it is harder to put new people in places of leadership and trust. I would say she has the lead."

"Very well," Antonia said. "Thank you all for your input. I believe we have three good potential Overlords in the competition. This could take weeks. Please consider the Overlords you know and how they handle their territories. We will reconvene once I call the competitors up. The doorman has notified me they are here. Please put on your cloaks and return to your seats."

Ten minutes later, the elevator doors slid open. The curtains had been drawn, so the room was dark, other than a half dozen wall sconces providing light. Antonia and her team were waiting in silence.

"Welcome back," she said. "Please join us at the table."

Jaroslaw stepped forward first with Eztli close behind. Kiona kept a casual pace, satisfied with being the third to arrive at the table. They took the chairs they had used before, with Jaroslaw in the center.

"I want to start by congratulating all three of you on your first endeavor."

Jaroslaw and Eztli exchanged a quick look.

"Establishing authority is important as an Overlord. This can be done through a combination of force, influence, and planning. A good mixture of these things is important," Antonia said. "The committee and I have discussed the events at the police precinct and have feedback for each of you."

She looked over her committee members and then the competitors. They all gave their full attention but did not speak.

"I'll start to my left with Eztli. You did a fine job collaborating with Jaroslaw on the raid. Your strikes were quick and effective. Creating a mess can lead to additional stress after the fight is complete, so being precise is good."

"Thank you," Eztli said.

"Jaroslaw, you are next. You used your quick connections to learn about the strike that the Dracs had planned. You communicated well with Eztli and worked with him to complete the effort. An impressive attack. The one drawback was that you have a clear affinity for slaughter. Your targets were not simply killed but eviscerated. This approach can be good in some settings and is unnecessary in others."

"So, I'm being docked points for making a mess?" Jaroslaw said with a slight edge in his voice. "You weren't even there."

"Calm yourself," Antonia said. "You must keep an open mind to succeed in this competition. I will remind you that there are no points. The committee will discuss events and decide the ultimate winner. Also, you would be smart to remember that just because you do not see us doesn't mean we aren't watching. Our power exceeds yours. Einar and Xue were both present at the precinct during the attack, although they did not assist in any way."

Antonia turned slightly in her chair to face the last competitor.

"Kiona, you elected a different approach to this event. You did not participate in the counterattack at the police precinct. In fact, you didn't go there at all. You did follow the other two as they watched the build-up to the Dracs' invasion. The fact they did not notice you was interesting. Then, you watched carefully and determined that someone away from the property was running things. You successfully tracked that to a van down the road. You had the least number of kills, but you had the most important one. Killing the leader of the attack is usually the best way to cause confusion and allow a window for gaining control. The one downside that Ahmed noticed was that you were caught on video, which was broadcast to the man who calls himself Count. Now he knows what you look like."

"Thank you for your feedback," Kiona said.

"I can sense the anxiousness from all three of you, so I will move directly to the feelings of the committee," Antonia said. "We are still very early in the competition and there is no definite leader at this point, however we will not consider it a tie. Kiona is in the lead, Jaroslaw is close behind her, and Eztli is right with him."

"She barely helped!" Jaroslaw said.

"Mind yourself," Antonia said, her eyes widening. There was a flare in her voice. "If you force me to remove you from this competition, I will do it. You will not like how that goes. The committee holds the final decision and will not be swayed by childish outbursts. Do you understand?"

"Yes," Jaroslaw said, suddenly looking small.

"Good. Now, you are all excused. We will alert you when it is time to convene again. Be diligent in your efforts, and know we are there watching," Antonia said and stood.

The rest of the committee and the competitors got to their feet. None of them spoke.

"Competitors, you are all dismissed. Please leave the tower."

They each offered a slight bow and went to the elevator. Riding down together, they kept their thoughts to themselves. Jaroslaw stared at Kiona, deciding he shouldn't express his feelings to her.

"See you next time," said the doorman.

Kiona watched as Jaroslaw went out into the bright sunlight and turned left. Eztli was with him. She went right, thinking that she could use a snack. Jaroslaw glanced back over his shoulder, to see her moving away.

"So, now we know," he said.

"Know what?"

"We know that killing the person in charge is all that matters. Whoever kills the Count will win the competition."

"That's what you took from what Antonia said?"

"What else could she have meant?" Jaroslaw asked.

"I feel like they are looking for a well-rounded approach. Kiona is winning, but barely. I'm not worried about her. Being sneaky is no way to run a territory."

"I suppose not. Still, I think killing the Count will go a long way to securing the win."

"I'm sure it will," Eztli said. "Maybe we should start tracking his movements a little closer."

"That's a good plan. I would like to keep working together, though. At least until it is no longer possible for the sake of the competition."

"That's fine with me."

18

"As a reminder, the driving range is closing at eight tonight for a private party. There is no rush to complete your games, but no additional time may be purchased this evening," said a man's voice over a loudspeaker. "Thanks again for visiting Super Golf this evening!"

The crowd had already begun to thin as the timers ran out on the booths. Wait staff hurried to clean up each one, anticipating the party that would be arriving soon. The bar started filling up with people in outfits displaying the Dracs emblem.

"Look at 'em," a short man with rosy cheeks said. He held a mug of Michelob Ultra and gestured toward a group in a booth. "Criminals! The lot of 'em."

"Let's go, Chuck," one of his friends said.

"I'm not done with my beer, and you know I'm right!"

"Is there a problem here?" asked a tall, slender man in a black vest with the Drac logo.

"You all are the problem," Chuck said.

"Sounds like the beer is talking," the Drac said, keeping his cool. He turned his attention to Chuck's friend and said, "I think moving along would be best."

"We're leaving."

"I'm finishing my beer and I have more to say," Chuck said.

"Here," said the Drac and took a ten from his jeans pocket. He snapped it open to make sure Chuck saw it. "I'll buy that beer back from you. Your friend can take you somewhere to finish off the night. Okay?"

Chuck started to respond, but his friend stopped him.

"Thank you," he said and took Chuck's beer. He set it on a vacant high-top table. Chuck grabbed the ten and spun away. "Let's go to O'Malley's."

"Have a good night," the Drac said. He watched them all the way out the door.

"I would've shoved that mug right in his mouth. He didn't need all those teeth," said another man in a Drac vest, who was approaching from behind.

"Yeah, but we have instructions not to make a scene here."

"True."

"Although, if you aren't busy after this, we know Chuck's name and that he's going to O'Malley's. We could drop by."

"Oh, I am always in for that. Ready for a drink?"

"Yes," the first Drac said and turned for the bar.

Dozens of Dracs milled about, paying little attention to the man in the corner in a black suit. He looked like a guy off the street, but he was also perfectly comfortable around the group. A woman in a red dress walked up to his table when he waved her over.

"Yes, sir," she said.

"Find out who that man is," the Count said, nodding toward the Drac who had just given Chuck ten dollars. "I want to interview him for a spot at the table."

"Very good, sir."

"Lucy. Have we seen any sign of the vampires?"

"Not yet, but they will be here. We put the word out to the entire city. They definitely know about it."

"I'm counting on it. Is Lance ready?"

"He's in a party room with Denise. She's almost done with his makeup."

"Excellent. You think he looks like me?" the Count asked.

"I'm confident that Denise will have him looking enough like you to draw them in. In fact, from what I saw, I think he'll fool most of the regulars. Until he talks."

"Good."

"Once we are ready for him to come out, I think you should leave. If things get messy, I don't want to take an extra risk," Lucy said.

"Fair enough. Is my driver out front?"

"Yes, Lloyd is out there, but he's in a gray Malibu. Your Cadillac should stay here to keep up the facade."

"Agreed."

Denise walked up to the table and gave a slight nod to the man.

"Lance is ready, sir. Would you like to see a picture?" she asked.

"That's not necessary," he said with a wave of his hand. "I trust your abilities."

"Thank you, sir. Should I tell him to come out?"

"I'll get him soon enough," Lucy said. "Thank you. Please enjoy the rest of the evening."

"I'm nervous for Lance," Denise said.

"Understandable," the man said. "We have a plan that will keep him safe."

Denise nodded again and walked away, blending back into the crowd.

"Let's not put this off any longer than necessary," he said, getting to his feet. "I'll be at the bank. Bring them to me. I want them all."

"We will do our best," Lucy said.

"That's fine, as long as your best is bringing me all the vampires. The black female is the one I want most, but there are at least two more."

"Yes, sir," she said.

The man took one last drink of his water, looked across the crowd, and went down the hallway to the main entrance. Once he was out of sight, Lucy went to the party room to get Lance.

The range was well-lit, and members of the group had started hitting. Balls sliced and hooked all over the wide, green space. Laughter rang from the tee boxes. At the far end of the range, an abandoned railroad ran along a berm five yards beyond the light. Two figures were on the back side of the berm, watching the party get underway.

"Do you see him?" Jaroslaw asked.

"No, but he'll be here," Eztli said. "We get him tonight, and it's over."

"So, our partnership ends here?"

"This is a massive gathering, so I think we'll still need to work together through this."

"And whichever of us happens to get the Count wins?"

"I've been thinking about your proposal and have a counteroffer."

Jaroslaw watched a dozen balls bounce out across the grass.

"Go ahead," he said.

"You want Chicago. Right?"

"Ideally."

"Ok. You had suggested a geographical division of the territory. I would rather have a division based on population first, keeping geography in mind. You can have Chicago and I'll start here. We can divide things evenly."

The golf balls offered soft pops as they hit the packed ground. The owners were smart, keeping the grass short to make people think they could hit it farther than they really could.

"I can work with that," Jaroslaw said. "Now, how do you want to handle this attack?"

"Let's go straight across the driving range. We can dodge the balls easily enough. By the time they realize what's happening, we'll have the Count."

"There he is."

Lance walked through the crowd, waving to the regular members of the Dracs. He was in the Count's full gear, although Lance was slightly taller than him. No one would say anything about that discrepancy.

"Let's give him five minutes to make his rounds," Eztli said. "He'll probably settle in at one location once he greets everyone. We can move in then."

"Seems easy enough."

"Too easy," said a woman's voice from behind them. They turned to look. "I mean, he's a sitting duck out there."

"What are you doing here, Kiona?" Eztli asked.

"The same thing as you."

"Jaroslaw and I are teaming up. I don't believe your help is needed."

"Oh, I wasn't offering," she said. "Your plan is terrible."

"Really?" Jaroslaw asked. "What would you suggest?"

"Not going after him here. This has all the makings of an ambush. Why give them what they want?"

"He's too arrogant to think we could get to him," Eztli said. "He has all his people around him. His plan must be to create a barrier big enough to stop us. I'll go through them like butter."

"Like butter?" Kiona asked. "Now who's being arrogant?"

"Just stay out of our way. We'll be in charge of this territory by tomorrow."

"Mind if I watch?"

"I don't care," Eztli said.

"Good," Kiona said. She walked along the back edge of the berm to a spot where a crooked tree had worked its way out through the old rip rap. She took a seat and waited.

Kiona watched patiently as the golf balls continued to fly. She was amused by the game in general. The Count had made his way to a long table near the center of the tee boxes. As soon as he sat down, she looked over at the other competitors. She wondered for a moment if she should jump in but decided against it.

"Go," Jaroslaw said.

He and Eztli raced out into the light in a blur that the golfers would only notice if they were trying to see them. It took less than ten seconds to traverse the range. They were close to the tee boxes when Eztli glanced down and noticed red beams. He attempted to jump over, but his toe caught one going up at a steep angle. Jaroslaw hadn't seen them at all, going full speed into them.

Nets shot out from small launchers from multiple directions. Both competitors were caught in them, but immediately began to tear themselves free. A dozen Dracs jumped up and aimed rifles at them. The shots rang out, driving four drugged darts into each of them.

Kiona climbed to the top of the berm when she heard the shots. She saw Jaroslaw and Eztli fight the nets for a mere ten seconds before collapsing. A team of gunmen stepped out to cover them, watching for more attackers.

Another group of Dracs ran into position, grabbing the two competitors. They carried them almost like pallbearers with coffins. Each team moved quickly through the building and into the hallway leading to the parking lot.

"Damn it," Kiona said.

She started running along the range, staying just outside the edge of the lighted area. She went through some brush and heard three more shots but knew they couldn't see her. The darts ripped into some trees well behind her.

When she made her way around the main building, she saw that there were dozens more of the Dracs in the parking lot. Most of them were armed with net launchers or rifles. She paused to assess the situation.

The two teams carrying her competitors came out the front door. A woman stood at the top of the stairs giving directions. Kiona considered taking her out but knew that wouldn't get her to the Count. She doubted that he was there in the first place.

A small, white box truck came bouncing into the parking lot after it cut the entrance too short and went over the curb. It swung into one aisle and then backed toward the front door. One of the Dracs rushed out and rolled up the back door. The first team put their captive inside. Kiona felt she had to act, but also knew she would be in that truck with them if she messed up. The territory would likely be hers if she let this happen.

"Can't do it," she said and ran for the second team.

A net flew by on her left and dart went to her right. She zigzagged through the crowd, grabbing the net-wrapped figure from the second team as the other one was tossed into the truck. Even more shots rang out and she heard the darts popping into the vehicles around her.

Kiona made it through the gauntlet that the parking lot had created. The neighboring building was dark, but she spotted a ladder leading to the roof. She hauled the body in her left hand up with her and dropped it near an air conditioning condenser unit.

When she turned to look back at the truck, she saw them pulling the door shut. There were people standing all around the truck, and other vehicles were lining up to accompany it. Shots were still being taken in the direction she had gone. She didn't think she could overtake that group on her own.

"Antonia and committee, if you are watching, please know that I'd go after him if I thought I wouldn't die in the process. If you can save him, do it. I don't mind the competition going longer. This is not how I want to win."

There was no response and the truck pulled away. Kiona reluctantly turned away and went to the one she had saved. She tore at the net over the face but could see it was Eztli. He had five darts sticking from him, so she plucked them out.

Once she had the net completely removed, she picked him up and jumped down to the parking lot. The crowd at the driving range was dispersing. Police sirens could be heard in the distance. Kiona elected to find somewhere safe for the night.

19

The box truck pulled into the Drac's garage next to the former bank building where the Count held his meetings. The driver took it to the back of the area and parked it with the nose two feet from the wall. Six people moved to the back of the vehicle and pulled the doors open. Helsing stepped forward from the group and looked inside. He tapped his phone.

"Sir, we have one."

"Only one?" said the Count. "I'll be right over."

"They are fully sedated."

"That's one thing they did right."

"Yes, sir."

The group stared at the bound figure with darts still protruding from various points on the body. The steel door at the side of the building banged shut. Those in attendance jumped because they knew the Count was close.

"Hesling," he said. Everyone noticed that he was in his full dress attire. "Let me see the face. Keep another round of darts ready."

"Yes, sir. Cut the net!"

One of the men in the truck took out a six inch knife and started sawing at one of the ropes. They were tougher than expected, but the Count maintained his patience. The figure's glove on their right hand twitched, drawing his attention. He shook his head, thinking that the glove was too big to be the black vampire he had wanted.

"White male," said the man with the knife as he pulled the netting back from Jaroslaw's face.

"Very well," the Count said. "Bring him to the box."

He turned away from the truck and walked between two cars parked perpendicular to the box truck. Helsing stepped past him at the last second to open the door leading to a room at the back of the neighboring building. The fluorescent lights came on, flickering as they warmed up.

Four Dracs came in three minutes later. They were carrying Jaroslaw's limp body between them using the net. His eyes were open, but he had a vacant look in them. Helsing pointed toward a chair along one wall.

"Put him there and secure him," he said.

"Is the camera ready?" asked the Count.

"Yes. We can be online in less than ten seconds."

"I want this one recorded. Broadcast it in an hour. I want to put the word out that the video is coming. This is a big day for us," the Count said.

"Yes, sir," Helsing said.

The Count walked to a folding table along the opposite wall from where they were securing Jaroslaw. He studied an arming sword that was resting on a black velvet blanket.

"We're ready, sir," Helsing said from his spot at the control panel. The Count turned around. "Lights up."

Three spotlights came on. They were aimed directly at Jaroslaw, but his head sagged, and his eyes remained dilated. The net still enclosed most of his head.

"Cut the bindings from above his shoulders," the Count said. "I want his face to be clear in the video."

The man with the knife from the truck was joined by a woman with another knife. They went to work cutting the net. The rest of the group watched as Jaroslaw's head came into view.

"He looks just like one of us," the man with the knife said.

"Don't be stupid," Helsing said. "He's not like us. He's a vampire."

"But he looks like one of us. Anyone on the street could be one."

"You'd know if you saw one."

"Enough," said the Count. He picked up the sword and gave it three waves. "This is plated in silver?"

"Yes. It's a steel sword that we had plated with silver," Helsing said.

"Good. Bring it to me when I signal," he said, placed it back on the table, and walked to Jaroslaw's left side. "This is where your life ends. We are more powerful than you and this broadcast will prove it. I would ask you to blink to show you understand, but I don't care."

Jaroslaw stared at the floor. His eyelids didn't move.

"Start the recording!"

Helsing tapped two buttons and held up three fingers. He dropped them one at a time and then pointed to the Count. A red light came on next to the camera.

"Greetings. I am the Count, head of the syndicate known as the Dracs," he said, staring into the camera. "This recording is being broadcast to prove two things. One, these beasts, that most would call vampires, are nothing close to the things described in books or movies. They appear to be like us but are simply another race that has attempted to suppress our growth for far too long. St. Louis moves out from under their shadow tonight. Two, the Dracs are now in complete control of the city. We have successfully overtaken a police precinct and have killed off vampires. No one can withstand us. We will continue recruiting and expanding our influence. Keep your eyes and ears open. Join us soon!"

The Count grabbed his head and tilted it back. He looked down into his eyes and smiled. He lifted his numb upper lip, revealing his fangs.

"See his teeth? Those with similar fangs have struck fear into the hearts of people for many years. As you can see," he said, smiling to reveal his own fangs, "I, too, have fangs. I do not fear this thing, but you should fear me. I have the desire to build an empire and I will do it. Do not get in my way."

The Count pointed at the table. One of the Dracs grabbed the sword and brought it to him. He lifted the sword and studied the blade.

"Now for the part that will remain with you for years, as a reminder of my power. This arming sword is plated with fine silver, which is well known to destroy these beasts. Watch as I end yet another of them. This serves as my final warning to the others who remain in our city. The Dracs control St. Louis!"

He held one of the edges of the sword to Jaroslaw's neck, who still didn't move. The Count gave a violent pull and the metal dug into the vampire's neck. Blood began to run down in thin streams. Jaroslaw twitched but could not fight back. The Count watched him bleed, but knew the wounds were not fatal. He bared his fangs one more time and thrust the sword into Jaroslaw's gut. He stabbed him another half dozen times.

Finally, Jaroslaw's head rolled back, and a low groan gurgled from his throat. The camera caught every instant of the killing, including the moment when Jaroslaw's body turned into a sort of cloud and drifted down, creating a thin layer of dust across the Count's shoes. The net fell to the chair. Everyone in the room stared. Helsing ended the recording.

—

Police Commissioner, Darryl Sisk, sat at his desk watching the video for the third time. His desk phone gave three short chirps.

"Yes," he said, after tapping the speaker button on his desk phone.

"We've got a half dozen reporters with crews out here," said one of the officers working the main entrance to police headquarters. "They want a comment."

Sisk muted the call and said, "Yeah, no shit."

"Commissioner?"

He opened the line and said, "I'll be down in the next ten minutes. We'll do it right there on the steps. Tell them to get set up. I'm not waiting around."

"Yes, sir."

He hit the End Call button. Then, he realized he was holding his breath and let out a long sigh.

"Get it together, D," he said to himself. "There's only one way to handle this, so go do it."

Sisk wore a suit most days, but he decided to change into his dress uniform for the interview. The reporters would have to wait, but he didn't care. He practiced his points as he swapped clothes.

"There he is!" said a Channel 5 crew member when Sisk came through the front door.

A podium had been moved to the top of the stairs. Navy blue velvet ropes hung between stainless steel posts to close off the area where the commissioner would be. Four officers positioned themselves evenly around the outside of the roped area.

"I'm going to start this off by saying we recognize this is a serious situation and that we are admitting that organized crime has returned to the city. However, we will get control of this mess. We will take down this gang and its leaders. They are common criminals who had the benefit of ambush attacks. They won't be able to do that again. The attack on the banks was well orchestrated, but we're already tracking suspects. Their murderous rampage through one of our stations was only possible because they outnumbered us and were willing to kill anyone they saw. Disgusting. Finally, we have this clearly doctored-up video of this Count supposedly killing a vampire. Stoker created a fine piece of fiction, but that's all it is. Now, I will be setting a more formal debriefing for you all as soon as we make some headway. No need to keep the switchboard lit up in there. Thank you," Sisk said.

He waved and turned back to the building. Reporters started calling out questions at him, but he kept going. He wanted a win before he stepped in front of the camera again.

—

Eztli's eyes snapped open. In the next instant, he leaped to his feet and moved to the corner of the room nearest to him. His vision adjusted to the dark space. Only a thin frame of light coming in around the curtain to his right broke the blackness. He sniffed the air.

"I can smell you," he said, taking another lungful of air. "Where are we?"

"Don't be so dramatic," Kiona said. "The door is ahead of you on the left."

He made his way to the door and carefully touched the knob. There was nothing abnormal about it, so he gave it a quick twist. The latch released and the door swung open, stopping when it hit the big toe on his left foot.

"Where are my shoes?"

"Next to the front door where you left them. Now, come out here."

Eztli opened the door the rest of the way and looked out into a hallway. It had lime green walls, brown carpet, and a globe with a single bulb in the center of the ceiling. He could hear the faint sound of a motor running in the room at the other end of the hall.

"Where are we?"

"I already told you that you have to come out here. Then, we can talk."

"Sounds like a trap."

"That's ridiculous," she said. There was a whoosh of wind and Eztli found himself looking her in the eye. "If I wanted you dead, I would have left you with The Dracs. Or, I could have killed you when you were passed out. Why would I wait until you are able to defend yourself?"

"I don't know."

"I'm going back to the living room. You should join me," she said and was gone. "Feel free to grab a bite in the kitchen on your way by."

Eztli felt more confident after giving himself a moment to think. He peeked around the corner and saw a woman's body stretched out on a dining table. The jeans had been partially torn off. The exposed area on the left thigh had a large section missing.

"Where'd you get her?"

"She came with the apartment. Now, hurry up. We need to talk and come up with a plan."

He walked into the kitchen and studied the woman's body. The center of her face was caved in, so he assumed Kiona had punched this woman as soon as she opened the door. There were three plates on a wire drying rack next to the sink, so he took one. Then, he saw the knife that Kiona had used, so he cut off an extra-large slab of meat from the untouched thigh.

He was disappointed that her face was ruined because he liked trying to guess what flavors might show up in a meal. He particularly liked Southern Europe and Northern Africa because the Mediterranean gave a slightly different note than other bodies of water.

"There's hot sauce in the refrigerator."

"What?" he asked.

"Hot sauce. Refrigerator. She's bland."

"Oh."

"Finally," Kiona said when Eztli sat on the couch perpendicular to the recliner she had chosen. She was watching some sort of auto racing but had little interest in it. "So, whatever they drugged you and Jaroslaw with was powerful stuff."

"Where is he?"

"He's dead."

"The Dracs?"

"Yes. Obviously," she said. "You two were reckless and ran right into their trap."

"Why didn't you save both of us?" Eztli said, cutting off another piece of meat and taking a bite.

"They already had him secured when I got there. Remember when I just said it was a trap?"

"Yes, I do."

"I'm going to need you to try using your brain more if this is going to work."

"I could take you anytime," he said. "You shouldn't insult me."

"If I thought you were a threat, I would have left you with the Dracs."

"I would have escaped."

"Just like Jaroslaw did?" she said. "Think about it. The only reason I'm not the Overlord for this territory right now is that I wanted to actually win."

"You think you can best me?"

"Probably, but at least it's a competition. I think we should team up like you and Jaroslaw were doing."

"Fine," he said, taking another bite. "To be clear, though, you only saved me so you could try to beat me?"

"That's accurate."

"I'm going to try to win, too."

"I'd expect that."

"What's your plan? I know you have one."

"I have recordings of the Dracs killing Jaroslaw, which was sent out as a warning to anyone who challenges them, and the police chief's press briefing about them. Finish eating and watch both. You two didn't do much planning, but I do a lot of it."

"I can do that. How'd you get this apartment?"

"Simple. You needed rest and I knew we'd both be hungry, so this apartment complex was an easy target. We're only two blocks from the driving range. The lights were on in this apartment, so I chose it."

"Random killing. Doesn't seem like you," Eztli said.

"It's only a human and one of us will be Overlord soon, so they belong to us anyway. She's food and nothing more."

"True. Can you play the videos?"

"Yes."

20

"Are you sure this is a good idea?" asked a man in his twenties standing across the street from the Midtown Theatre. It had once been a busy venue, but new and modernized options had pushed it aside. "I didn't even know this place was still open."

"Dude," said his friend. "You need to pay attention. Remember when I bought Bitcoin when it first came out?"

"You tell us about it all the time. Too bad you didn't keep it."

"I was twelve."

"What does Bitcoin have to do with this?"

"You gotta get in early on good things. We saw that video of them killing a vampire. They took down an entire police precinct. This group is the real deal."

"There are cop cars at both ends of the block. What about them? I saw the police chief saying they were going to strike back."

"He's just posing. They got nothing on a grassroots thing like this. If they could do anything about it, they'd have done it already."

"I guess," the first man said. "Let's go in, if we're going in."

"Right on," his friend said.

They checked for traffic and stepped into the street. Two sets of doors in the theater stood open. A pair of people stood at each entrance wearing vests with the Dracs logo.

"Welcome to our recruiting event," said a woman, as they approached. "We're happy to have you. Go on in and find a seat. It's about half full right now, and we're asking people to stay on the orchestra level."

"Thanks," said the second man. "Metal detectors or anything?"

"Not here," she said. "We encourage weapons, and we all work together. How else will you defend yourself and the rest of the Drac family?"

"Fair point," he said, and they went inside.

Another dozen people had lined up behind them. The average age was under thirty, but there were some older people in the crowd. The two men walked down the center aisle, glancing at a pair of people in stocking caps. One was a black woman, the other a Hispanic looking man. The two men kept walking.

"We're drawing too much attention," Eztli said. "It's not the right weather for these hats."

"You worry too much," Kiona said. "There are lots of people wearing them. It's a hipster thing."

"We're hipsters?"

"Are you that dense?" she asked. "Never mind. We don't stand out, but we're at a recruiting event for the Dracs. People are going to look around. Curiosity is a powerful thing."

"Curiosity killed the cat."

"I should have let them kill you."

"That's no fun," he said. "Have you seen the Count?"

"Not yet, but I'm sure he'll be here. No way he misses this."

"If he shows up, I'm going to kill him."

"You need to watch what you're saying," Kiona said. "If one of these people hears you, they'll out us."

"And we'll kill them, too."

"See, this is what I warned you about. You and Jaroslaw were reckless."

"Are you telling me you're in charge now?"

"I'm not in charge, but I made the plan for tonight. If you don't follow it, I won't save you again."

"I won't need saving, but I'll go along for now."

Kiona didn't respond. Instead, she slowly scanned the room. Dozens of people wearing Drac vests were in small groups from one wall to the other. There was still no sign of the Count. She saw one of the Dracs at the right end of the stage look at her and quickly look away. She didn't like that.

"Hey, they're starting," Eztli said, giving her a slight jab in the ribs.

"Yeah, I see that. Keep your eyes open. Something is about to go down."

"The Count is going to die. That's what's about to go down."

"Do you know how to have a thought without verbalizing it?"

"What do you mean?" he asked.

Two lights directed at a podium at center stage came on. Kiona didn't bother answering his stupid question. A man built like a model for a big and tall store walked casually out from stage right to take his spot in the light. He looked over the crowd for a minute with a pleased expression on his face.

"Welcome," he said. "My name is Helsing. I serve as the right hand to the most powerful man in St. Louis. No, the most powerful in the region. Soon, he will be the most powerful in the country!"

The crowd cheered. He drank it in.

"Thank you! Now, I want you all to know how happy the Count is to have this good of a turnout. We have seventy-seven current Dracs, not including those of us on the Count's council. At the last report, we have passed the century mark for recruits. That is outstanding and we are happy to have you all."

The clapping started again, but he waved them off.

"We will celebrate later. Now, we need to talk about one of the biggest parts of joining our organization. Completing a task that furthers the agenda of the Count and the Dracs is a critical step in being admitted. You all are lucky because you don't have to wait to perform something for the Count."

Helsing raised his right arm and then held it out in front of him with his finger pointing into the crowd. Another pair of spotlights came on. They searched for only a second before settling near the back, directly on Eztli and Kiona.

"What the fuck?" Kiona asked softly.

"Friends, we have been gifted not one, but two of these so-called vampires! These two are working to kill our beloved Count, which is why he is no longer in the building. You will meet him soon enough. However, your first task, should you choose to accept, will be to eliminate these two. There are no rules. Just kill them."

"Merda," Eztli said and jumped to his feet.

Kiona stood, turned to look at the entrance, and saw that a dozen Dracs stood in her way. They were armed and taking aim. A group of recruits were to her left, trying to decide what to do.

"Let's do this," she said and launched herself toward them.

"Oh my god!" yelled one of the men in the group, but that was all he had time to say.

He brought up his fists to fight. Kiona was on him like a rabid dog. She immediately ripped his chest open, flinging chunks of meat in every direction. Four other people stepped in to grab her, while most moved back along the crowded rows.

She left her first mutilated victim on the floor and turned to face the people who had latched on to her. Her eyes narrowed and her fangs appeared through her smile. Blood sprayed from the severed neck of one of them when took his head off. She threw the wayward head toward the Dracs at the entrance.

They sidestepped, allowing the recruit's head to smack against the stone floor before rolling away. One of them leveled his gun at her and started shooting. The others joined in.

Kiona ducked out of the way. Three other recruits and one Drac weren't so lucky. She felt the warm spray of their blood and smiled, realizing they were willing to kill their own to have a chance at her. She glanced back to where Eztli had been. He wasn't there. The bullets stopped flying overhead.

"He's over here," said one of the Dracs. "Shoot him!"

Eztli knew what had to be done, but he was also furious over the death of Jaroslaw. This led him to grab the first Drac and tear his arms off. The man's mouth formed a scream, but nothing came out. Nothing except some foamy blood when he started to convulse.

Before he could hit the floor, Eztli grabbed the two women that were next in line. The second one brought her gun around faster than he expected, but he grabbed it and kept it moving in the arc she had started. When she pulled the trigger, her fellow Drac's head erupted into a chunky slime on the wall above the doors.

Eztli killed the rest in that line before anyone could come to their aid. Kiona locked in on the nearest group of Dracs to her. Opting to be more efficient, she tore out necks and sliced open guts. The screams of terror and pain echoed through the theater. Most of the remaining crowd began fleeing for safety.

Helsing and the rest of the council that were in attendance had slipped out a side door. The Count was already back in the bank basement, watching the slaughter. He was drinking whiskey, resisting the urge to smash his glass against the wall.

Over half the recruits scrambled out the different exits. Kiona and Eztli weren't worried about them. If anything, those people would tell what they had witnessed. That might deter others from joining the movement.

"Spare us!" a man yelled to Eztli.

He pulled off his Drac vest and tossed it away. He held up his hands in surrender. His eyes begged for mercy.

Eztli paused, but then said, "No."

Only three regular Dracs survived the night. They only managed that because they had been assigned jobs away from the crowd. Thirty of the recruits also died, most had been torn apart in a way similar to how an apex predator prepares its prey.

"Come out with your hands up!" said a woman through a loudspeaker outside the entrance to the theater. "This is the St. Louis Police Department, and we have the building surrounded. You have one minute to respond!"

"What do you want to do?" Eztli asked. "Kill them, too?"

"No," Kiona said. "Let's go out the top across the roofs. One of us will want some sort of police support once we become Overlord."

"Fine," he said and looked at the two balconies at the front of the building.

They leaped up to the first and then the second. Kiona glanced back down at the carnage and felt like they had made their point. The Dracs weren't going to win that easily. Both competitors went out a steel emergency door in the ceiling at the back corner of the top balcony.

21

"Yes," the Count said into his phone. "I need you to be here by midnight. I will give you more details then but be prepared to take your next step in your Drac career."

He tapped the screen to end the call and placed it next to his drink. His council chambers were empty, but he appreciated the calm. The sconces had red, flickering lights that looked like candles burning. A single square of ice rested at the bottom of his glass. His whiskey was back in his office, but he waited until his work was complete for the evening.

"My lord, we're back," Helsing said when he stepped into the room. "The others that were at the recruiting event are waiting in the antechamber."

"Good. All of them?"

"Yes, well, almost. Myself, Bram, and Lestat. Akasha and Gabrielle will be here before long.

"What was their delay?"

"They attempted to help fight the vampires, even though I ordered them back here. I will let you handle their decisions."

"Indeed," said the Count. "Did you see Lance and Denise?"

"I was not aware they were coming tonight."

"My question was whether you have seen them."

"Sorry, sir. I have not seen them this evening."

"They should be here in a matter of minutes. Make sure they are able to get inside and that they have access to this room."

"Are they joining us for tonight or permanently?"

"That is irrelevant to you at this time. Follow instructions, Helsing."

Helsing nodded before leaving the room.

At five minutes until midnight, there was a knock at the door.

"Enter!" the Count said.

"You wanted to see me, sir?" Lucy asked, closing the door behind her.

"Why weren't you at the recruiting event?"

"Helsing didn't ask me to be there."

"I see. What were you doing?"

"Nothing so exciting as a recruiting event, I'm afraid. I was picking up some cash drops from some spots around town and preparing deposits."

"Good," the Count said. "Have you been in my office before?"

"Once."

"Go to the tall, black cabinet in the back corner. The bottom drawer is unlocked and contains a collection of my favorite guns. There is a Glock 19 at the far left end of the row. It is loaded. Bring it to me."

Lucy went through the door at the back of the chamber and into his office. Two lamps were on, but they did little to help her negotiate the room. The black cabinet absorbed what light the room held. She opened the drawer and removed the gun. The Count hadn't moved when she walked back into the chamber.

"I'll take it," he said and held out his left hand.

Lucy handed it to him and moved to the far end of the long table. He gave the slide a gentle pull to check for a round in the chamber. Once confirming it was empty, he slid it back all the way and loaded the weapon.

"Go tell Helsing to bring everyone in."

"Yes, sir," she said and went to the hallway leading to the antechamber.

Helsing led the way back into the room. Lucy returned to her regular spot at the tail of the line. The Count noticed her looking at his gun as soon as she stepped through the door. The others, except for Lance and Denise, took their seats.

"Welcome to my council chamber," the Count said. "Your recent work, along with some unfortunate vacancies, has led me to choose you to serve on the council. It can be stressful and dangerous, but the rewards make it all worth it."

"Thank you, sir," Lance said.

Denise nodded after her nerves kept her from producing words.

"Tradition requires that you each select a handle or nickname to use rather than your real name. This keeps an extra layer of protection around the Dracs and me. I appreciate names selected from a favorite vampire-related book. However, I will not look down on you for selecting something from a movie. Please choose one now and your legal name shall never be spoken in my presence again."

"Count, sir, I would like to take the name Carmilla, if it is available," Denise said, surprising herself with how quickly she delivered that thought.

"Carmilla?" the Count asked and raised his left eyebrow. "I have to say that I am impressed. Not enough people are familiar with that title. The name is approved. You will have the sixth chair on my left side, Carmilla."

"And you?" the Count asked, turning his gaze upon Lance.

"I would like to go by the name Blade."

"Ha! Blade?"

"Yes, sir."

"Lucy, what kind of council member has the name of a vampire hunter?"

Lucy thought of the gun and quickly considered the best way to answer the likely rhetorical question.

"Sir, our names don't actually mean anything. They are a code name to help with communication."

"In the future, I would like more levity from you, Lucy. This situation is obviously a joke. We have to make sure the new additions feel like part of the team."

"Right," Lucy said. "I'll do my best."

"Now," the Count said, "you want to use the name of a vampire hunter when we are vampires. Is that right?"

"Technically, he is a blend between humans and vampires who only hunts full-blooded vampires."

"Sir."

"What? Oh, yes, sir. Sorry, sir."

"Fine. I approve of the name," the Count said. "However, it puts ideas in my mind. Don't let me find you hunting the wrong vampires."

"Sir, I would never do that, sir."

"One 'sir' per sentence is sufficient," he said and ran his finger around the top of his glass. "The reason you are all here so late is that we had a situation this evening. I need to be debriefed. Helsing, were you in charge?"

"I was, sir. We had a turnout of about forty higher than expected. We had no issues with security, the police, or the venue. I think we were all pleased…"

"Shut the fuck up!" the Count yelled. His face was flushed, but he showed no signs of the fury hidden just below the skin. "You dare to sit here at my right hand and tell me you had no issues tonight?"

"I only named three things. You didn't let me…"

"Just stop! I'm done with excuses. I watched the entire thing. Plenty of pageantry, that's for sure. We knew the police wouldn't start the fight, so there was nothing to plan for on that front. Finally, I selected the venue based on the needs I perceived for the effort. Two of your three kudos had nothing to do with you. The third one bragged about security. You must be fucking kidding me to think security did anything right."

The Count slid his chair back, considered his next words, and stood up. His left hand rested on the gun. He let out a sigh. Then, with a flick of his wrist, he grabbed the gun and brought it up to shoot.

He shot twice, adjusted to the right, and shot two more times. The pop of the gun echoed around the room, while people ducked and looked for safety. Splinters from the doors on the cabinets at the far end of the room sprayed out at those closest to it.

"Get up," he said.

The council members peeked over the edge of the table at him. One by one, they returned to their seats. Akasha dusted some pieces of the cabinet off the table in front of her.

"I'll ask you all to turn your attention to the cabinets. As you can see, there are the remains of two pictures hanging there. Those are the two vampires that are causing us trouble. There is no reason we can't eliminate them, yet they are still out there."

He looked from person to person around the table, finishing with Helsing.

"So, I have to ask a question, but I already believe I know the answer. How in the actual fuck did they walk into the event without so much as a notice being sent out?"

Helsing said, "We did…"

"Don't talk!" the Count yelled again. "I wasn't done. We know exactly where one of them is at all times. The other one is likely close by. You were all able to lock down their spot in the theater and then pick them out with spotlights. However, no one thought to kill them. This takes us back to the pageantry."

"Sir," Helsing said, interrupting again. "We wanted the Dracs and the recruits to take them down. I thought it would be a great story."

"You thought it would be a great story. Interesting. Instead of it being a great story, it turned into the worst possible story. How are we possibly going to get a good turnout for a recruiting event again now that word is out that we are vulnerable? Don't answer that. The police that responded now see that we have a weakness. That's all Chief Sisk will need to move forward. Can I assume the tracking device in the male vampire is still active?"

"It is," Helsing said. "We've been keeping an eye on him since the driving range."

"You had all the tools you needed, but still I'm looking at a massacre that we lost. We lost because we let them win. Is that right?"

"There is more to it, sir. I didn't want to risk shooting into the crowd."

"Bull shit! I watched on the feed when your security team opened fire once the vampires had gone on the attack. They killed some of our own and never got close to the target."

"Taking the shot to kill the target is hard."

"Is it?" the Count said, turning to look at his right hand man. "I don't see it that way."

Without another thought, he raised the gun and pointed it at Helsing. There were three quick shots, splattering the big man's brains and pieces of his skull across the wall behind him. The Count lowered the gun and put two more shots in Helsing's chest. Jaws dropped, but no one dared to move.

"Lucy," he said.

"Yes, sir," she said, staring at Helsing's ruined head.

"You are familiar with the tracking software. Correct?"

"I am."

"Good. I am promoting you to my right hand effectively immediately. How do you want to handle this?"

"We've been drawing them to us," she said. "Perhaps we should go get him. If they are together, we can kill them both. At the very least, we cut their number in half."

"Going on the offensive seems like a good way to use the tools we have."

"I can take a team with me and handle it."

"No team," the Count said. "I want you and two people of your choice from this group to do it. We will show our ranks that we have more power than they believe. Executing a third vampire will prove that."

"I'll take Bram and Carmilla."

"Are you ready for that, Carmilla?" he asked.

"I am, sir," she said.

"Don't come back without a corpse, Lucy. Two would be best. Lestat and Blade, clean this mess up. If the chair is ruined, dispose of it far from here."

"Yes, sir," Lestat said.

"Meeting adjourned," the Count said.

He looked at his gun, picked up his whiskey glass, and went to his office. The rest of the council jumped to their feet, but he didn't bother waiting to see what they did. Lucy looked at Helsing once more before walking out of the room. Carmilla and Bram went after her.

As the Count poured a fresh glass of whiskey, Eztli was slicing another piece of meat from the woman in the apartment. It was getting old, and some flies were swarming around. He figured it would be good for one more meal, at least.

"Where are you going?" he asked when Kiona came out of the bedroom she had been using.

"I want something to eat," she said, pulling the hood of her sweatshirt over her head. "That meat is no good. The flies are settling in."

"Tastes fine to me," he said.

"You do what you want," she said. "I'll be back in a while."

"Bring me something?"

"I'll call you before I come back to see if you are still hungry."

"Fine, but I'll be hungry. Your comments are making me lose interest in this."

"Then, come with me."

"I'm going to watch this show," he said. "Maybe we ought to find a new apartment soon. The neighbors will be complaining about the smell soon."

"Smartest thing you've said all day."

"We're only thirty minutes into the day."

"Bye," she said and went out the door.

The apartment complex wasn't far from a walking path, so she took it. There wouldn't be anyone out exercising, but she had a feeling there would be something good along the way. She drifted along unnoticed until she heard voices coming from a grove of old trees. She sniffed the air. Marijuana.

"Dinner and something to take the edge off," she said.

Back at the apartment, Eztli picked at his meal. A fly landed on it, so he set his plate on the couch next to him. Two California Highway Patrol officers on motorcycles were pursuing a sedan on his show. It was an older show, so the driver of the car pulled over after a minute and surrendered.

"Boring," he said, and flipped the channel.

A knock came at the door. Eztli sighed and muted the shopping channel he had landed on. Seconds later, there was another knock. He got up and made his way to the door. He leaned in to look at the peephole. A woman in a plain black shirt and jeans was standing outside. Her head was turned to the left.

"He's there?" she asked.

Eztli stepped back, realizing something wasn't right. In that instant, bullets ripped through the door. Lucy had taken an M16 from the weapon cache at the bank. When her weapon clicked empty, Bram and Carmilla dropped in from either side with their own weapons and continued shooting.

The vampire's body had been pushed back against the side of the archway leading to the kitchen. Eztli crumpled to his knees when the shooting stopped. His body was shredded in places, but he fought to move out of sight.

Bram kicked the ruined door open, and they went in. Carmilla marched directly to Eztli, who tried to lunge at her. He fell short. She took out a pistol and emptied it into his skull. He offered one last groan and turned into dust. The bullets that had been in his body clattered to the ground.

"We don't have a corpse to bring back," Carmilla said.

"It was symbolic. He's killed two of them and knows exactly what happens," Lucy said. "Let's go."

Kiona had surprised a group of college students in the woods. They fled when they saw her, but one of the men had just taken a big hit and stumbled. She easily snatched him up and bit into his jugular. The sound of heavy gunfire in the distance grabbed her attention. She did not release her meal, but she listened.

"Eztli," she said into the man's pulsing neck.

He stared up into the trees, trying to process what was happening. She released her hold on him, frowned, and snapped his neck. He was delicious and she wanted to make sure he'd be there when she got back.

"It better not be him," she said, getting to her feet.

She walked out of the trees, preparing to race back to the apartment.

Suddenly, two figures appeared in front of her. They were blocking her way. It only took a moment for her to realize who they were.

"He's dead," Xue said.

"What?" Kiona asked.

"Eztli is dead," Einar said. "Antonia has had us watching you the last few days. Your instructions are to be at the penthouse at seven this morning. The competition is over. Congratulations."

"No one was watching over Eztli?"

"Ahmed and Jiemba were watching him," Xue said.

"Then, why didn't they help him?" Kiona demanded.

"That is not how this works, and you know it," Einar said.

"Finish your meal and find a new place to spend the rest of the night. The desk attendant will be ready to admit you at exactly seven. Do not be late."

The two of them vanished. Kiona thought she saw them go back toward the apartment but wasn't certain. She considered going to check on Eztli. Instead, she followed Antonia's instructions.

22

"Ah, good morning!" said the doorman, as he pulled open the first in a bank of glass doors. "Five minutes early."

"Yes," Kiona said, stepping through the door. "Punctuality is important."

"You'll make a lot of friends across the territory with that mindset. Congratulations, by the way."

"Thank you," she said, looking at the sealed elevator door. "We still have some things to attend to today, but hopefully this will be my territory soon enough."

"Gossip travels fast, especially in St. Louis. Word has it that the other competitors are dead. That means you win. Right?"

"Technically, yes, but I need to speak with the committee first."

"Are you going to turn it down?"

Kiona turned her head slowly, making eye contact with him. She was not impressed with his question. He could tell he had reached the end of that line of discussion.

"My apologies," he said, walking back behind the desk. He tapped some keys and waited. "The elevator should be down in a moment. They are ready for you."

"Thank you," she said, turning to face the stainless steel door. When it slid open, she felt a wave of anxiety slam into her. Internally, she fought to take the steps forward through the inclination to run away. The doorman thought she looked like a statue.

He was about to tell her it was ok to go up again when she stepped inside. The red velvet interior blended well with tastefully sized mirrors and dark oak trim. The elevator started to climb on its own, so she turned to face the front. She knew the committee was already watching her.

"Welcome," Ahmed said, as soon as the door was open. "The committee is eagerly awaiting you."

"Thank you, but I need to address the committee before we get started."

"You want to go first?"

"I need to make a request."

"Interesting," he said and glanced back at the others, who were already at the long table. "I'll ask Antonia. Stay here."

He strode directly to the spot opposite Antonia. A frown formed at the corners of her lips while her brow furrowed.

"What is it?" Antonia asked.

"She wants to make a request of us before the ceremony begins."

"Postpone being named an Overlord?" Xue asked. "Was she injured?"

"She seems fine to me," Ahmed said. "I'm curious as to what this could possibly be. Has this ever happened before?"

"Let's check the statistics later," Antonia said. "The Queen will be calling before long. She will expect us to be at her part of the ceremony."

"She'll also expect us to be recommending someone who wants the position," Jiemba said.

"Fine," Antonia said. "She can make her request, but we need to keep things moving."

"Join us," Ahmed said, after turning to face Kiona.

Kiona took a deep breath, exhaled, and walked across the room. Ahmed moved around to his chair on the other side of the table. She stood behind the center chair, gripping the top of it hard enough to cause a squeak in the wood.

"Welcome, Kiona," Antonia said. "You have earned the title of Overlord and this North American territory. However, as I understand you have a request, we will hear from you before beginning. Keep in mind that Queen Stephanie will be calling soon. We won't keep her waiting."

"Yes. Thank you. I have one request of the committee this morning. I understand that, according to the rules, I am the winner. In some ways, I know I bested them. However, I know that being an Overlord requires the ability to lead others and show them what you expect from them," Kiona said, taking a breath. "The Count was a bigger threat than originally thought. He killed my predecessor, Kenny McClelland, and both of my competitors."

"And your request is?" Antonia asked.

"I am requesting a delay in this ceremony until I can deliver the head of the Count to this committee."

"Perhaps all of this hasn't quite sunk in yet," Einar said. "Once you are named Overlord, you will have soldiers at your disposal. You can eliminate any challenger with little more than the lift of a finger."

"Eventually, I might try that approach," she said, as the left corner of her mouth curled up. "Now, I want to show any potential soldiers, advisors, other Overlords, and even Queen Stephanie, what kind of leader this territory has."

"Again, you can do all of that after being named Overlord," Einar said.

"I want to win this competition. This feels like it fell in my lap."

"That is hardly the case," Antonia said.

The phone on the table next to her rang. A white, flashing light appeared next to the top button on the console. Antonia studied Kiona for another second before tapping the button.

"Good evening, my queen," Antonia said.

"Good morning, Antonia," the queen said in a youthful voice that belied her age.   "Are you and the team ready for me, I hope?"

"My apologies, Your Highness, but we had a development in the minutes leading up to your call."

"Is the candidate still there?"

"Yes, she is."

"Then, what seems to be the problem?"

"Kiona has made an unusual request."

"An unusual request on her first day? Do tell."

"I'll let her explain," Antonia said and gestured toward Kiona. "Go ahead."

"My queen," Kiona said, suddenly feeling her throat tighten. "I know that I have already won the competition by the rules, but I would like more time to win it on my own. Simply outliving Jaroslaw and Eztli is not good enough for me."

"These competitions and the rules that govern them have been occurring for millennia. What is it that you want to accomplish that can't be done as Overlord for that territory?"

"I don't seek to change the traditions involved in this process, Your Majesty. I want to seek out and kill the leader of the group causing problems here. I understand that I will have any number of options to make that happen once I accept the position, but I think this act sets me up for a better beginning to my time here."

"Hmm," the Queen said. There was a full minute of silence before she continued. "I can appreciate your reasoning for this. However, this is not a game to me. I will show great leniency and give you two options."

"Yes, ma'am," Kiona said.

"First, you can complete the ceremony now and assume the title of Overlord. Use your network and eliminate these nuisances. I have read Antonia's updates and feel like it has taken longer than it should have. Second, you can delay the ceremony. However, there will be conditions. You will have six days from the time this ceremony was to have begun, so the time is already drifting away. You will kill this delusional human and deliver his remains to the committee. If that happens, then you will become Overlord. If not, then you will lose your claim to this territory and you will never be permitted to compete again. What do you choose?"

Kiona stared at the phone. She was partially surprised the Queen had agreed in any way, but the conditions made it hard to want to go that route. She would be risking a life of luxury to prove a point.

"Well?" Antonia asked after what felt like only a second or two to Kiona.

"My Queen," Kiona said, "I will deliver this man's remains. I accept the risks involved and look forward to continuing this process in the coming days."

"Fascinating," the Queen said. "Your request is approved. You have less than six days. I suggest you begin your efforts immediately. Antonia?"

"Yes, ma'am."

"You and your team will stay there for six more days. As soon as that time period expires, you are all free to return to normal life. Your additional efforts in this competition will be duly noted."

"Thank you, ma'am."

"Until next time," she said and hung up.

Antonia looked up at Kiona. The rest of the committee did the same. She went from being nervous to feeling the weight of her decision.

"If it's okay, I would like to get started."

"Queen Stephanie suggested that you begin immediately, so you certainly should. This ceremony is canceled. You are free to go."

"Thank you," Kiona said.

"I hope to see you again within the allotted time. Good luck."

Kiona offered a half bow, turned around, and went to the elevator. She knew they were watching her go and couldn't wait to get out of the building. The doorman offered a tip of his cap on her way out but didn't say anything.

Once she was on the sidewalk, she drew a deep breath and looked to her left. This had seemed like a good plan an hour ago. Now, she wondered if heading off to take a nap as Overlord would have been the better option.

A block away, she saw three people in Drac vests crossing the road. The potential of killing them because she could entered her mind. She waved it off because she knew she had to stay focused. Only the Count mattered, and she would find him soon.

23

"Fuck my life," said a young woman with black hair and bright red lipstick from behind the counter at Steve's Coffee.

"What?" asked the man next to her as he poured milk into a cup while preparing the next drink.

"I have to work until eleven and it's a quarter after seven. I've barely been here an hour. Plus, it's nice outside."

"Yeah, well, life's a bitch and then you die."

"So true," she said and tapped her earpiece. "Welcome to Steve's. What can we make for you today?"

She rolled her eyes and faked gagging herself after completing the mandatory greeting. The customer started his order. Neither of them noticed Kiona at a small booth in the corner nursing a cup of black coffee.

Kiona was listening until the woman said it was after seven. One day had elapsed since she made her request. The previous night had been utterly fruitless, but she planned on being more aggressive on day two.

"Hey," said a man from Kiona's right. "I think that's her."

"Dumbass, why would a vampire be sitting here drinking coffee?"

"I don't know, but it looks like the woman in the picture they texted out today," he said and took out his phone. Kiona sat still. "Here. You tell me."

"A grainy surveillance picture. Yeah, she's black but way hotter."

"Hotter?" the first man asked. "Vampires aren't hot. They're scary as fuck."

"I wasn't talking about the vampire. Watch me work," he said and walked over to Kiona's table. "Mind if I sit?"

"I'm not looking for company," she said.

"Boyfriend?"

"No."

"Okay, then," he said and sat down across from her. "My name's Trevor."

"That's rude," she said.

"Anyone ever tell you that you look just like Zoe Saldana?"

"No. Now, leave me alone."

"Gotta let a guy shoot his shot, right?" he said, offering a wink and a smile. "It sounds like you have a bit of an accent, but I can't place it. I guess you aren't from St. Louis?"

"I'm not, but I might be moving here soon."

"That's excellent news. Well, it's lucky that you're meeting me today."

"Why is that?"

"See this vest? It means I'm part of the Dracs. We run this town."

"You do? A political group then?" she asked.

"Not exactly."

"So, you must be one of the bosses."

"Not yet, but I'm on my way up."

"Ah, you're a guy in a vest then."

"Now who's being rude, cutie? What's your name?"

"You don't need to know."

"Look. I need you to work with me here," Trevor said. "One of the other guys is here with me."

"You want to use me to show off?"

"I mean, no, not exactly. You really are good looking."

"I'm surprised you don't have women chasing you down."

"I know," he said, glancing back at his partner. "Can I take you to dinner this weekend?"

"I doubt our menu choices would overlap."

"Are you a vegan or something?"

"No. Not a vegan."

"Okay, then. We'll be fine."

"I'm going to pass. I need to get to work," she said and slid to the edge of her seat.

"How will I get a hold of you?"

"You won't."

"Hold on. I have an idea. Meet us for drinks this afternoon. There will be more Dracs there and you can see what I'm talking about. They know I'm a rising star. I'll buy."

"How generous of you," she said and glanced at the other man in the Drac's vest. "You're persistent, for sure."

"Like that's bad?"

"What bar?" she said, thinking that surrounding herself with more Dracs could improve her chances of learning something.

"You'll be there?" Trevor asked.

"How could I resist?"

"Are you messing with me?"

"Too many questions in a row. I'm going to go," she said and stood up.

"Wait, no, we'll be at McMahon's Irish Whiskey Bar. It's in the Central West End. If you give me your number, I can text the info to you."

"I know how to look it up. What time?"

“Everyone should be there by three.”

“Fine. I can always go for good whiskey. I’ll judge the company later.”

“Challenge accepted,” he said and stood up. “Can I get a hug?”

“No. Don’t make me wait this afternoon.”

“I wouldn’t dream of it.”

Trevor took a half-step toward her, but she spun and went out the door before her absence registered with him. He shook his head and sighed. His friend joined him.

“She hooked you pretty fast.”

“Aiden, my man, I’m in love.”

“Gross.”

“She’s going to meet us at McMahon’s this afternoon.”

“Bold move.”

“Why?” Trevor asked.

“We’re going to be talking about Drac business at some point. You’ll have to send her packing.”

“Maybe I’ll recruit her. She has a sort of a goth vibe. She might be down.”

“Whatever you say, Rico Suave. I’ll see you there. I want to get an early nap. It’s going to be a long night and I had to do some collections early this morning.”

“I told her we’d be there by three, so I’ll shoot for two-thirty.”

“I’ll be there at three,” Aiden said. “Later.”

—

“I thought your girlfriend was coming?” Aiden asked when he returned with a Jack and Coke.

"She'll be here and don't call her my girlfriend," Trevor said. "I think I've got a shot with this one. Don't fuck it up for me."

"Oh, I don't think we'll be the ones to fuck it up," Aiden said, looking at the other three guys at the table.

They laughed.

"Assholes. All of you."

"Could be worse," Aiden said and took a drink.

"So, what's the plan for tonight?" Trevor said. "Not sure if my lady friend will be interested."

"Interested? Why the hell would you tell her in the first place?" Billy asked. "This is for Dracs only. It's not a recruiting event."

"Calm your tits, big boy," Trevor said. "If she wants to join, then I'll take care of the paperwork before the meeting."

"Moobs," Nate said, giving his drink a twirl. "I think that's the preferred nomenclature."

"What?" Billy asked.

"I think moobs is what you big boys prefer. Isn't it? An abbreviation for man boobs."

"Eat a dick."

"I'll leave that to you."

"Can you two shut the fuck up? Jesus," Trevor said. "She's going to be here any minute. I'm sure of it."

"Uh huh," Aiden said. "I'll buy a round if she shows."

"Good. I've been trying to get you to buy a drink for over a year. Now, for tonight, they are starting at seven. Right?"

"Yes. At the school," Nate said. "Pretty sure we're not supposed to be talking about it in public though."

"The old South Middle?" Billy asked.

"Do you want to go ahead and make a flier?" Aiden asked. "Make plenty of copies, so we can give them to everyone here."

"Smartass."

"No. For real. You're a dumbass. The vampires are probably listening, and you just gave out the name of the one place the Count had kept secret for sure."

"Calm down," Trevor said. "We'll drop it. Everyone knows where we're going."

"Where are we going?" Kiona asked, stepping up to Trevor's right elbow.

"Oh, hey," he said, turning to greet her with a hug.

"No," she said, putting a finger in front of his face.

"He shoots and misses!" Nate said from the other end of the table.

Trevor shot him a look and the others enjoyed a laugh at his expense.

"Easy now, boys," Kiona said. "My apologies for being late getting over here. I did a shot with the bartender and had a good chat about my favorite whiskey."

"Jack?" Aiden asked.

"Oh, definitely not," she said. "Double Jameson with one cube of ice."

"All right, I can let that go. I owe the table a round. Are you good? Uh, what's your name? Trevor?"

"I didn't get the chance to ask," Trevor said, blushing.

"Kiona is my name, and I will be ready for another drink by the time you get back."

"Not a lightweight, then."

"Far from it," Kiona said and took a sip. "Hurry up."

"I like her," Aiden said, getting down from his stool. "Be right back."

"So, where are we going?" she asked. "I just got here."

"Well, it's a thing for the Dracs. I was going to ask you to join us, but maybe that would be too fast."

"You didn't even know my name and you were going to ask me to join your club?"

"It's not a club," Nate said. "More like the mafia. We run this town."

"So, I was told. I'm still new here, so I can't make a commitment like that yet."

"But maybe eventually?" Trevor asked.

"The future is full of surprises," she said.

—

"Hey!" said a woman on her porch across the street from the old South Middle. "Are you one of the new tenants?"

"No, I'm not," Kiona said, standing on the sidewalk in front of the school.

"Good. Can't believe they're turning that place into apartments or condos or whatever they call it these days. It was a good school. My kids went to school there fifty years ago. Now some yuppies want to move in? No thanks."

The sun had set, so only the last light of dusk let Kiona see her. She was wearing a plain yellow sweater with powder blue sweatpants. An ashtray sat on top of the porch railing next to her. The faint glow at the end of her cigarette came to life and then faded.

"Here for the party then?"

"I think so. They didn't call it a party, though."

"Not sure what else it would be. I saw a bunch of people in Halloween costumes. They always go around back to the old gymnasium. Most of them were wearing that stupid patch I saw on the news for those vampire people."

"They are not vampires. I can assure you of that," Kiona said, looking at the building.

"Well, whatever they are, they are a pain in my ass!" the woman said and took another drag from her cigarette.

"Why are they a pain?"

"They show up for these parties every once in a while. They park wherever they want, and they sit around making noise all night. One of them pissed in my shrubs last month."

"I see."

"Yeah, well, if you're going to the party, then you are probably friends of theirs. Don't come shit on my porch or something later."

"That's not my style and I wouldn't say I'm a friend of theirs. I only met five or six of them today."

"I'd hop back in your car and go home if I were you."

"I appreciate that. Maybe I'll go in and see what's going on."

"Suit yourself," the woman said.

She took another puff and then smashed the butt out in the ashtray. Kiona watched her get up, grab her cell phone, and go inside without saying another word. That was fine because she had work to do.

Kiona retraced her steps to follow the sidewalk back to the corner and then turned to go along the side of the building. She glanced over her shoulder just as the woman's house went out of view. She figured that the woman would watch her as long as possible.

"Who the hell are you?" asked a man in a Drac vest when Kiona rounded the back of the building.

"Oh, I'm here for the meeting."

"What meeting?"

"The one that's going on inside. I was invited by Trevor."

He looked her over.

"I don't know Trevor, but you're hot. Give me a kiss and I'll let you go in."

"I'm not doing that. I can smell your breath from here."

Three other men in Drac vests started laughing. Kiona saw that one of the doors leading inside the gym was propped open. She wanted to wait until the last possible minute to give them notice of her arrival.

"Quit fucking around, Junior," said one of the other men. "The meeting starts in two minutes. Let's go in. If she knows about it, then she's supposed to be here."

"I guess," Junior said. "Find me afterward."

"I will do my best," Kiona said and smiled, but did not show her teeth.

"Good," he said and went for the door.

The other three were six steps ahead of them. When Kiona got inside, she found herself near the back of the room. Basketball goals were bolted to the concrete block walls and the gray tile floor still had lines painted on it for different activities. She was surprised to see how full the room was.

The stage at the end of the room had heavy, red curtains. Kiona chose a spot along the back wall to wait for her chance. She didn't see Trevor or the others but thought that was for the best.

"Welcome!" said Lucy as the curtains parted and slid to each side.

The crowd cheered, paying no attention to the fact Lucy was addressing them instead of Helsing.

"It is wonderful to see you all here tonight. We have some great news to share, and you get a special treat tonight. The Count is here!"

The group cheered again. Kiona clapped along, but still drew attention from those nearest to her. She nodded to them, hoping to put them at ease.

"I will start by saying the Count plans to tell you all about the plans he has to expand the territory controlled by the Dracs. Now that we have more money coming in and an established presence, we can grow. Who's ready?"

More cheers.

"The police will not challenge us, and we have killed three vampires! They won't bother us again. They know we will win. Their time is in the past! Now, without further ado, I present the Count!"

Everyone stood up straight, clapped, and screamed their approval, as if they were at a concert. Kiona tensed, knowing her time was near. She could smell the adrenaline and cortisol in the air. A quick scan of the crowd revealed people on stands near each side wall holding guns.

"Hello, my faithful friends," the Count said, stepping from the shadows.

He held up his hands and drank in the excitement. All but one of the guards looked toward the stage, wanting a chance to see their leader. Kiona knew it was time.

She stepped forward, pushing between two women in Drac vests. In the next few seconds, she split through the crowd like a shark's fin in the ocean. She heard two loud pops and people screaming just behind her. The crinkle of the nets like they had used on Eztli and Jaroslaw registered as they entangled Dracs instead of her.

"Vampire!" called one of the guards close to the stage.

He started shooting, but his motion was much too slow to keep up with Kiona. She shoved the last few people out of the way and leapt onto the stage. Members of the council stepped up to create a sort of barrier in front of the Count.

"Excellent!" he said. "Another vampire for me to kill!"

In the split second after he finished his thought, Bram's head was detached from his neck and landed in a thud at the Count's feet. Kiona had a grin on her face with her fangs showing. The Count returned his own fanged smile.

He drew a silver dagger, still believing that silver would stop a vampire. Kiona barely looked away from him but managed to rip open Carmilla's chest and throw her guts to the ground. Lestat's face turned to shreds in an instant beneath her fingers.

The others tried to close in around her, except for Lucy. Kiona noticed she was retrieving some sort of rifle from a table behind the curtains. Kiona's plan had been to attack quickly and end the competition.

The Count swiped at her with his dagger. She easily grabbed his wrist with her left hand and squeezed. Her right hand grabbed him by the neck. She looked up into his eyes.

"You don't have what it takes," he said and swung his left fist up to punch her.

Instead, she crushed his larynx and tore out his throat. Blood sprayed from his freshly opened carotid arteries. His head tipped backward, holding on by a section of tissue.

There was a bang to Kiona's right. The flash of Lucy's gun lit the corner of the stage. Kiona stepped forward, allowing the drugged dart to go an inch behind her and into the crowd. It would strike a teenager halfway to the back. The dose would nearly stop the teen girl's heart, but that was a mercy compared to what everyone else got.

Kiona grabbed the Count by the hair and gave a vicious twist. The last of the tissue from his throat ripped, sounding like wet denim being torn in half. His body fell away. She lifted the Count's head into the air.

"Kill her!" said Lucy.

Seven figures appeared at the foot of the stage. They were facing the crowd. Those in front had started toward the stage, but quickly backed off. Another five were on the stage, addressing each of the Council members.

"Antonia!" Kiona said.

The olive-skinned vampire strode in through the back door. The Dracs stared in disbelief at the woman in a pearl-white gown. Her outfit alone cost more than everything the Dracs in that room were wearing. She reached the stage and hopped up with little effort.

"A good evening to you, Kiona."

"And to you. I had a feeling you would be following me."

"There is not much else to do at this point."

"The others didn't come along?"

Antonia said, "I think you have something for me."

"In fact, I do," Kiona said. "I thought I had to present it at the tower."

"I don't want that mess in the building. Keep it as a trophy, if you wish."

"What's the next step?"

"We will convene at seven tomorrow morning to complete the ceremony. Then, I get to go home. You can do whatever you please. You are an Overlord."

"An Overlord," Kiona said, appreciating the situation for the first time. "Who are all the rest?"

"They were advisors and soldiers for Kenny McClelland. Once they heard what was happening with the competition, they offered assistance. I told them they couldn't do anything until you had that thing's head."

"Now what will you have them do?"

"I am not in charge of them. You are. What do you want them to do?"

"Kill them."

"Interesting choice. All of them?"

"They had a chance."

The crowd began to buzz with confusion and panic. Some started toward the double doors at either back corner. That's when the doors were torn from their hinges and tossed aside. The other four members of the committee came in. Another dozen commoners were behind them.

"I am Kiona, Overlord of this territory. I have personally dispatched your leader and this organization is now eliminated. I'm only telling you all this because I want you all to know you lost. I want you to feel that pain."

"Kiona!" said a man to her left. "Spare me and my friends! We were nice to you."

"Trevor," she said. "I have to say that I would not be standing here right now, if it wasn't for you. You didn't know who I was and let your hormones run wild."

"So, you'll let the five of us from today go?"

"Oh, Trevor, no. None of you are leaving on your own!"

"We'll fight!" Trevor said.

"Please do. It makes it more fun for us," Kiona said. "Kill them all!"

The vampires swarmed into the room like sharks finding a school of mackerel. Each council member received a deep bite on the neck, as they transitioned into a snack. Lucy still held her gun, her eyes locked with Kiona.

"A double dose might kill you. Even if it doesn't, I can still make you hurt."

Lucy leveled the gun and closed one eye. Her finger had only brushed the trigger when Antonia appeared next to her and drove the first two fingers of her right hand up through Lucy's jaw and into her brain.

"No. You won't," Antonia said, watching Lucy shiver and die. "My outfit is ruined."

"I can reimburse you," Kiona said, stepping up next to her.

"Reimburse me? My dear, no. I haven't paid for clothes in at least a thousand years or more. I can get another just like this with a simple request."

"I do appreciate you helping me with her."

"You didn't need my help, but I have been on my best behavior this whole trip and thought I deserved an indulgence," Antonia said, glancing back at the bloodbath. "Enjoy your evening. Celebrate. Do what you want, but don't be late for the ceremony at seven."

"I will be there and ready to move forward this time."

"Good evening, Kiona."

"Also, to you."

24

At ten minutes after seven the next morning, the white, flashing light next to the top button on Antonia's phone started flashing. She looked up at Kiona and nodded.

"Hello, my queen," Antonia said.

"Hello, Antonia," the queen said. "Good day, everyone. I'm pleased to be speaking with you all today. I have been updated on the events from last night. Congratulations, Kiona, on completing the task in a timely manner."

"Thank you, ma'am."

"The transition from one Overlord to the next is usually a bittersweet time. Hans or, most recently, Kenny McClelland handled this territory like few others could have. As you know, it is one of the last original territories on that continent. I chose to leave it intact for a while longer. The amount of work for the position has escalated over the past few centuries, requiring more delegation and trust in your team. Sadly, your predecessor was undone by trusting the wrong assistant a little too long. All positions within your territory are yours to fill. Most of those that worked for Hans are continuing the day to day operations while you prepare to be their new Overlord. It is not unheard of to sack the entire group and that is up to you."

"No, my queen, I know things are running quite well outside of St. Louis. I don't see a reason to break something just to fix it."

"Very well. As your queen, I'm available for conference, if you want. Please get to know other Overlords and do your best to be active in their network. We are a team. Now, I don't want to drag this out. I, Queen Stephanie, hereby recognize Kiona as the new Overlord for this territory. Her appointment is effective immediately. All territory holdings and monies will be made accessible to her as soon as possible."

"Thank you, my queen," said Kiona.

"You have earned this, but your work has only just begun," the Queen said. "Antonia, I thank you for your work on this competition. Einar, Xue, Jiemba, and Ahmed, I know you all played a big role in the success of this competition. Take a month to relax before returning to work."

"That's very generous of you, Your Highness," Antonia said.

"Yes, yes," Queen Stephanie said. "Kiona, I look forward to what you will accomplish with this territory in your new role. I have another meeting soon, so I must conclude this one. Goodbye."

There was a click and the sound of an open line before anyone else could speak. Kiona looked up from the phone to see the committee watching her. She felt a smile form on her face and knew this was real. The committee stood and clapped.

"Congratulations," they said in turn.

"Thank you."

"And thank you for that smorgasbord last night," Einar said. "It was light on the salad, but the meat options were exquisite."

"A win for everyone," Kiona said. He nodded. "I had hoped Celia would be here for this. I understand, though. It could be emotionally challenging."

"Understand? Oh, no," Antonia said and looked at Einar. "Celia isn't here because she is pursuing revenge. She's not missing this because of emotional concerns. "I think you should visit her at some point. You will learn a lot about, shall we say, stoicism."

"I see," Kiona said. "Then, with my first official act as Overlord, I invite you all to join me for a drink. I found a good little neighborhood place that starts serving early."

"So be it," Antonia said. "This ceremony is complete."

—

The sun sank toward the Pacific Ocean off the shore of Costa Rica, creating beautiful purples and reds across the sky. Three men were stretched out on chaise lounge chairs, looking west at the water. The little cabana they had rented provided shade during the hot days and a place to party in the evenings.

"Anyone need a drink?" asked one of the men. He was slender and pale, which made him appreciate the cabana even more. "I'm going up to the bar."

"Yeah, I'll take a hurricane," the man in the middle said, lifting up his empty glass.

"Are you buying this round, Paul?" the slender man asked.

"I'm paying for the cabana and the room. You can pay for a dozen damn drinks, Craig."

"I paid for all the drinks yesterday," said the third man. "Food, too."

"Don't oversell it, Jace," Craig said. "That surfer didn't cost you anything."

"Just get the drinks, Craig!" Paul said.

"Jace Smith?" said a woman walking toward them across the sand.

She wore a sheer cloak over a one-piece bathing suit. Her hair was pulled back into a ponytail. She looked Mediterranean and all three men stopped to watch her approach.

"I'm Jace. Who are you?"

"My name is Celia."

"Cute name for a cute lady," Paul said.

"That's disgusting," she said. "Sit down, Craig."

"What? I was about to get drinks. Do you want something?"

"Oh, yes, I want something, but they don't have it at the bar. Sit."

"Look," Paul said, "I can tell you're one of us. What do you want?"

"Are you Paul?"

"How the hell do you know our names?"

"That's a yes," Celia said. "Craig, if you don't sit down, I'll put you in the chair."

Craig laughed. Celia did not. He sat.

"I'll keep this short because I have places to be. Central America isn't one of them. I think you all know my son, Hans."

"I don't know anyone named Hans," Paul said.

"That doesn't surprise me," she said. "I will never understand how you convinced him to make you a deputy."

"Wait, your son is Kenny?"

"I am not a fan of his assumed name, but yes."

"Shit," Craig said.

"What do you want?" Paul asked.

"What do I want? I want your head on top of a wall for all others to see. You allowed the disease that was the Dracs to flourish in St. Louis and thus brought about the death of my son."

"It's not my fault they killed him."

"I think it was your fault. Shoddy work and lack of attention to detail. He made you rich and I'm surprised to see you wasting it at a very basic resort rather than something more upscale."

"How'd you find me?" Paul asked. "I've only been using cash."

"Why do you think I asked for Jace when I walked up?"

"No clue."

"Jace did me the favor of using a credit card with his name on it yesterday to pay a tab at the bar. A group of people helping me locked in on that transaction in a matter of seconds."

"You're a fucking idiot, Jace," Paul said.

"I didn't have any cash on me at the time and didn't feel like going back to the room."

"So, Paul, you now understand how having incompetent people working for you can be dangerous," Celia said. "The good thing for you is that Queen Stephanie gave me permission to punish you, but not to kill you."

"Kill me?" Paul said. "I think it would be a good fight, but I doubt you could kill me."

"Really?" Celia said with a sparkle in her eyes.

"I think you should stop talking," Jace said.

"Shut up, Jace. It's your fault she's here at all."

"Smarter than I thought," she said. "I appreciate that favor and it will save your life for now."

"Oh," Jace said.

"You should go. Get your things from wherever you are staying and leave. I won't be hunting you down, but it would be best if I don't come across you in the future."

"I understand," he said and stood up.

"Where do you think you're going?" Paul asked.

"She said I should go. I'm going."

"Coward," Paul said.

Jace shook his head and walked off toward the resort. Paul watched him go and then turned back to Celia. Craig was still focused on her.

"What now?" Paul asked. "You aren't allowed to kill me, so we skirmish and go about our lives? I will let you get in some good shots, and you feel better. Is that about right?"

"Not exactly," she said.

"Then, what? You can't think you can beat Craig and me at the same time."

"Actually, yes, I do think that. It won't even be that hard, which is disappointing."

Paul got up from his chair and took up a boxing stance. Craig stayed in his spot.

"Let's do this. I don't like to fight women, but you've got this coming. I did my job good enough and…"

Celia took three quick steps and punched him in the gut with enough force to drive him back onto his chair. Craig turned to the side as one of the arms splintered off toward him. Paul looked up at her.

"That was a cheap shot," he said.

"Then do something about it."

Paul leapt up and launched himself at her. She could see every moment of his approach and sidestepped his attack. As his fist flew into the place where her face had been, she grabbed his wrist and twisted it behind him. His elbow snapped under the stress.

"Aahhh," he yelled as his momentum carried him out into the sand.

He went down face first, unable to catch himself with his good arm. Craig got up. Celia turned to look at him. He was unsure but took a step toward her.

"Bad idea," she said.

She met him mid-stride and drove her fist through his face. His skull fractured, sending splatters of blood across the back wall of the cabana. Celia didn't give him another thought as she pulled her hand free. A sliver of skull cut the side of her finger.

"Ouch," she said, taking a second to look at the cut. "I'd kill you for that if you weren't already dead."

Paul groaned and tried to get up. He never got the chance. Celia jumped on him like a wild dog. She tore at his ribs and back, pushing him further into the sand. He struggled to fight back, but it was no use. Shock soon set in, as she tore away layers of flesh and then some organs. She was covered in blood and gore from her face down to her knees. Finally, she stopped to catch her breath and admire her work. The vacationers on the beach had stopped their walk to stare at the attack.

"I suppose I'll have to ask forgiveness from the Queen," Celia said and raced back north along the beach before anyone could get a good look at her.

About the time that Paul took his last breath, the doorbell on Marie's apartment rang. She had been watching television with a glass of wine, but checked her phone to see who it was. Brewster raised his head from his spot on the back of the couch to look at the screen.

"Who is it?" she asked through the app.

"Kiona."

"Oh, shit, sorry. I'll be right there."

Marie ran to the door with Brewster close behind.

"Hello," she said after swinging the door open.

"Hello," Kiona said. "Can I come in?"

"Yes, please do. It's a bit of a mess. I haven't had company yet."

"Don't worry about that, although it looks immaculate."

"Can I get you something to drink?" Marie said, closing the door.

"That would be nice. Red wine if you have it."

"I'm actually working on a bottle of that right now. I'll get another glass."

Kiona took a seat facing Marie, who filled the glass and handed it over. Baxter went back to his spot on the couch, but he sat up and watched the guest closely.

"I'm always happy to have you as a guest," Marie said, "but I'm assuming you are here on business."

"A little of both. Celia told me that you were Hans' top aide."

"Yes, Kenny and I had a great relationship."

"Right, Kenny. She didn't like that name she said."

"True, but she also didn't like him being in America. She's more traditional and wanted her son to take a spot in Europe with her and his father."

"I see," Kiona said. "I'm sure it was just her way of being protective."

"I'm sure it was. So, what can I do for you?"

"I'm hoping we can reach an agreement. I'm quite new to the area, having lived most of my life in Africa and Asia. My goal is to keep things going just as they were under Kenny, other than St. Louis."

"That's a good idea."

"I understand that Kenny left you a sizable fund and this apartment, so you don't really need to work."

"True."

"However, I would like to hire you as my top aide with a ten percent increase over whatever Kenny paid you. I know you know more than anyone else in the territory, so working for me would be a great help, even if it is temporary."

"I haven't had enough time to get bored yet," Marie said. "This was Kenny's apartment and his cat."

Brewster looked at her disapprovingly.

"Yes, well, I don't want either of those things. I will set up a new residence in each of the major cities."

"What about St. Louis? You aren't going to bring back Paul, are you?"

"Oh, no, I don't think that will be an option. Not that I would want him as part of my team."

"A good choice," Marie said.

"Should you accept my offer, I will rely on you to start handling communications from me to each of the deputies. If you can help find a new deputy for St. Louis, that would be great."

"Hmm. I hadn't given much thought to what I was going to do next. I did hear about the way you finished up the competition. I liked that."

"Thank you," Kiona said.

"I'll do it, at least for a while. Can we start tomorrow? I'd like to finish my movie and this wine."

"Tomorrow it is."